ALL IN

BOOK NINE IN THE SLEEPER SEALS SERIES

LORI RYAN

ALSO BY LORI RYAN

The Sutton Capital Series

Legal Ease

Penalty Clause

The Baker's Bodyguard (A Sutton Capital Series Novella)

Negotiation Tactics

The Billionaire's Suite Dreams

The Baker, the Bodyguard, and the Wedding Bell Blues (A Sutton Capital Series Novella)

Her SEALed Fate

The Sutton Capital Series Boxed Set (Books One Through Four)

The Sutton Capital Series Boxed Set (Books Five Through Seven)

Cutthroat

Cut and Run

Cut to the Chase

The On the Line Series (a Sutton Capital Spinoff)

Pure Vengeance

Latent Danger

Wicked Justice (coming soon)

Heroes of Evers, Texas Series

Love and Protect

Promise and Protect

Honor and Protect (An Evers, TX Novella)

Serve and Protect

Desire and Protect (coming soon)

Cherish and Protect (coming soon)

The Canyon Creek, CO Series (with Kay Manis)

Born to be My Baby (coming January, 2018)

Never Say Goodbye (coming February, 2018)

Thank You for Loving Me (coming March, 2018)

With These Two Hands (coming May, 2018)

I'll Be There for You (coming June, 2018)

If That's What it Takes (July, 2018)

Triple Play Curse Series

Game Changer

Game Maker

Game Clincher

The Triple Play Curse Boxed Set

Standalone Books

Stealing Home (writing in Melanie Shawn's Hope Falls Series)

Any Witch Way (writing in Robyn Peterman's Magic and Mayhem Series)

ACKNOWLEDGMENTS

You guys know that writing a book takes a village, right? I can't thank the people who step up for me enough. This was a blast to write! Thank you Natasha Bajema and Paul Jimenez for helping me with the technical and science side of this book. Scott Silverii, PhD., thank you for helping me when my characters were trapped in the woods. Elizabeth Neal, Bev Sten, Sara Smith, and Paris Vachon-Harris, thank you for proofing the final document for me! You guys are fantastic.

As always, any errors or creative license are my own. Please don't blame these guys!

PROLOGUE

Retired Navy Commander Greg Lambert leaned back in his chair and swallowed down the last of the one glass of bourbon he'd allowed himself that evening. He'd started to cut back lately. Vice President Warren Angelo's words echoed in his ears as he glanced at the clock on his office wall. It was time to make his next call.

"A sleeper cell of SEALs," Warren had said nearly eight months back, "to help us combat terrorist sleeper cells in the US... and whatever the hell else might pop up later."

Lambert rubbed at the spot in his gut that seemed to burn nearly all the time now. Warren had never had to tell him this would be black ops, the kind of thing that would never be documented on paper and would be denied if anyone ever got wind of what they were doing. Taking this on had its rewards. It had given Lambert a sense of purpose again. He'd tapped a number of former Navy SEALS to thwart terrorist threats around the nation, and each had been successful in heading off untold danger and destruction. On the whole, the mission he'd been tasked with could only be deemed a success.

But the stress of racing against the clock in a near constant state of high alert was taking its toll. Hell, between that and living his days out with his dead wife's Chihuahua who hated his guts, Lambert's quality of life was downright peachy. He ran his hand around the rim of the empty glass before turning it upside down next to the single sheet of paper on his desk. At least the bourbon was some of the best small batch money could buy. He wasn't a wealthy man, but he believed if you were going to put poison into your body, you might as well spring for the best damned poison you could get.

He had a SEAL in mind to take on this latest mission. He just hoped he would take it on. Luke Reynolds had been out of the teams for eight years. But the timing might be right to pull him back in. Not back into the SEALs, of course, but into the life.

Lambert hoped like hell Luke agreed. This mission bothered him more than most. Not because it was more heinous or had the potential to do more harm than others. They all had the potential to take lives, to destroy. This one was no different in that sense.

This one, though, had a level of greed to it that bothered him. Most of the time, the nut jobs they dealt with believed in what they were doing. They believed in a cause or a religion, something, other than the all mighty color green. The assholes who had thought up this scheme couldn't care less who they hurt. They wanted money and they'd do anything to get it. Twist anything and destroy anyone to get what they wanted.

The intel they had collected showed they were likely looking at a team of three people, possibly four. Greg opened his desk drawer and took out a bottle of Mylanta, looking at it before putting it back in the drawer. Who wanted to screw up the aftertaste of a good glass of bourbon with that chalky shit, even if he did need it?

He tossed a treat at the growling Chihuahua, hoping it would shut its yap long enough for a conversation. A friend had said the dog would learn to love him if he gave it treats more often. He had a feeling nothing could make it love him, but he'd never give him away. Karen had loved the little purse demon.

Greg placed the call that would get the ball rolling. It looked like this group would be holding their auction soon, and this was one sale that couldn't go through. Not on his watch.

CHAPTER ONE

"Have you heard from Naomi?"

Luke Reynolds looked at his brother as they crossed the road to the sandwich shop. They didn't have a lot of time for lunch since Zach was on the job, but they needed to talk. "Yeah. I talked to her a couple of days ago. She's still not thrilled with either of us."

Zach had the decency to look chagrined. "We probably went a little overboard," he finally said, as he held the door open for Luke.

Luke ordered their usual sandwiches while Zach grabbed them two bottles of iced tea apiece and a family-sized bag of chips for them to split.

Luke answered as he paid the cashier and the two moved down the counter to wait for their lunch. "Yeah." He scrubbed at the bristle covering his jaw. He needed to shave. "Maybe. I don't know."

He replayed the scene from a week back in his head. As soon as he'd seen the way those college assholes had looked at Naomi, he'd known they should have insisted she attend an all-girls school. Or stayed home and attended school locally. Or stayed locked in her room forever.

He looked at Zach. "We've been that age. You know as well as I do what those assholes were thinking as soon as they saw her. Hell, they were practically lined up along the sidewalks watching for fresh meat, and drooling while they did it. It didn't hurt anything for them to know she's got some muscle at home ready to defend her."

Zach hadn't raised Naomi the way Luke had, but he was almost as defensive of her. Sadly, raising his niece from the age of ten had taught Luke his gut instinct where she was concerned wasn't usually the right one. He'd gotten a lot of things wrong where she was concerned. She was usually more patient with him than any parent had a right to expect. But judging by the look on her face when she'd heard Zach and Luke growling at the male students when they'd dropped her off for her freshman year of school at Dartmouth College, he probably should have curbed his gut instincts.

He hadn't.

"But she's okay, otherwise?" Zach asked, grabbing the bag offered by the woman behind the deli counter with a nod. They walked outdoors and sat at one of the few small tables lining the sidewalk outside the deli, taking a few minutes to open their food and dig in.

"Yeah." Luke spoke around a large bite of turkey and cheese on whole grain bread. "Says she got into the classes she wanted and she likes her roommate so far. How's Shauna?"

Shauna and Zach had been dating for several months and Luke had to admit, he liked her for Zach. She was strong and sharp and just what his brother needed.

The goofy look on Zach's face could have answered for him. "She's good."

"She move in yet?" It seemed the next logical step for the pair, but Luke wasn't sure if Zach realized just how far gone he was for the woman.

Zach shrugged. "Soon. So, you gonna make it a habit to show up here for lunches?" He leveled Luke with a look. It wasn't every day that Luke showed up at the New Haven Police Department where Zach was a detective to drag him out for lunch.

Luke shrugged.

"You know you're like a housewife suffering from that empty nest shit, right? I mean you get how pitiful you are, right?"

Luke bounced a pickle off Zach's forehead, but it only earned him a laugh from his brother. He wasn't going to tell Zach he'd caught himself singing *House at Pooh Corner* the other day. That had been Naomi's bedtime song when she was younger.

Hell, he still sang it to her on occasion, but it was better Zach not know that he'd started singing it to himself since she moved out. That would give Zach fodder for taunting him for decades.

Zach was right about one thing, though. Luke didn't have a clue what to do with his life now that Naomi wasn't at home. Now that she didn't need him the same way she had.

Leaving the SEAL teams hadn't been easy for Luke, but it had been the right move for Naomi, who'd lost everything in one split second of stupidity.

Luke saw Zach's movements slow until his brother was staring at him, no longer eating.

Zach's voice was low when he spoke. "What's up?"

Luke chugged his first iced tea before opening his second. "I might be out-of-pocket for a little while. Just didn't want you to worry if I'm not around much." He and his brother had gotten used to seeing each other often since Zach made it a point to visit Naomi at least once a week, if not more. With the job he'd just taken on, that wouldn't be as likely. Luke would be keeping a low profile, and stopping by the precinct to see his detective brother wouldn't really fit with his assignment.

Zach tried to play the moment off as a joke. "I know you're not heading back to the teams. You're too damned old for that shit."

Luke grinned, giving Zach the levity he'd been looking for. "I can still swim circles around your tired ass, little brother." They both knew as a former SEAL, Luke could beat Zach in anything having to do with water.

They continued eating in silence for several minutes before Zach spoke again. "Anything you can tell me about?"

He had to know the answer, but Luke gave it to him anyway. "No."

"You got anyone watching your back?"

Luke shook his head, no, and rolled up the paper his sandwich had come in, ignoring the curse from Zach.

Zach looked around. There were plenty of people walking by their table, but none were paying attention to their conversation. "So, you're pulling a one-eighty? Going from safe and sound and no risk to throwing yourself into . . . into what?"

Luke didn't answer. Since their mother, sister, and brother-in-law had died in a car accident that stole everything from Naomi, Luke had taken the safest path he could find in life. He'd chosen to work running background checks instead of accepting any number of offers to do private security work or attend the police academy the way Zach had after his own separation from the military.

Zach continued. "She went off to college, but she still needs you. She still needs to know you're not putting yourself in the line of fire."

"Says the man who came home from the military to work as a cop." Luke couldn't help but feel some resentment. He'd never in a million years go back and change what he did when his sister and mom died. He'd never regret taking Naomi. Family was family, and you gave everything to family.

But that didn't change the fact that Zach had been able to do things Luke had felt he couldn't do. Zach hadn't played things safe the way Luke had. He'd been there for Naomi, same as Luke, but not in the quite the same way. He wasn't the one Naomi woke up to when she had a nightmare or relied on when she was sick or scared. Zach hadn't taken on being mother and father, as well as uncle.

"Look, Naomi will always be my top priority. Always. That doesn't mean I can keep sitting at home while she's . . . " He let that die out. If he finished the sentence with *while she's off living life* like he wanted to, he'd sound like a royal wuss. But it was the truth. She was starting to build her own life independent of him.

Zach had his own life. He had a career. He had purpose.

Luke had a business, but it was a business he'd been doing as a placeholder and it had always felt that way to him. He'd been running online background checks for people. Things couldn't get any safer—or more boring —than that.

He wasn't going to run off to fight a war, but the job he'd

been tapped for wasn't one he could turn his back on. Too much was at stake for that.

Zach must have read the look on Luke's. Luke wasn't willing to discuss the issue further. Zach sighed. "Just know I've got your back if you need me. You might think you're working this one on your own, but that won't ever be the case, you got me?"

Luke grunted and tossed another pickle, hitting Zach square between the eyes and earning a grin.

CHAPTER TWO

Lyra Hill hugged her brother as they stood on the front steps of her apartment building. With her on the step above him, they were almost the same height. "You're a lifesaver."

He shrugged but the accompanying grin was cocky. "Eh, no biggie. I love hanging with my girls." He turned to the four-year-old twins currently hawking the front door of the building waiting for someone to open the heavy glass and let them in.

When her boss had called her in on a day she should have been working at home, her brother had saved her by taking Alyssa and Prentiss for the day. They were likely sugared up, but she'd been able to get to the office for a few hours. According to the rundown Alyssa had given Lyra at warp speed upon their return, they'd convinced him to take them to the park followed by a trip for ice cream. Not just ice cream in a cup or a cone the way she would have. Real ice cream sundaes with double cherries and hot fudge. And, as Prentiss had put it with her nose all crinkled in the look she usually reserved for spinach, "no nuts."

The girls got their wish for the umpteenth time that day when Mrs. Lawson from 1C came out and held the door for the girls so they could scoot in ahead of Lyra.

Lyra rolled her eyes at Billy as the girls raced into the building and around the corner out of sight. She normally had a rule they had to stay in her line of vision, but they knew that rule wasn't applied very stringently in the apartment building. The neighbors kept an eye out on the girls.

"I better catch up to them." She waved as he walked away and turned to follow the twins.

Mrs. Lawson fanned her face. "Prepare yourself, honey. Hot and steamy hunk in there. I think he might have melted my glasses."

Lyra's feet slowed. "Huh?"

"You'll see." Mrs. Lawson gave Lyra a look as she continued to fan herself. "I've always hoped maybe you and my Murphy would get together, but even I have to admit he can't compete with *this*."

Mrs. Lawson walked away before Lyra could formulate an answer. She was a little stuck on the idea of her and Mrs. Lawson's grandson, Murphy, together. Mrs. Lawson had never mentioned that, and Lyra could honestly say she'd never once gone there in her own head. Not that there was anything wrong with Mrs. Lawson's grandson. He was just so . . . well, so . . . nice. And tame. And, well, boring, if Lyra really thought about it.

Not to mention, he hadn't once seemed interested in her. In fact, she thought he might be gay, but they'd never talked enough for her to know for sure.

"Huh," Lyra said, again, this time a statement instead of a question and very much to herself as she followed the girls inside since Mrs. Lawson hadn't bothered to stick around long enough to explain anything.

Holy Mary Mother of . . . The thought plain petered out in Lyra's head as her brain melted. At least only Mrs. Lawson' glasses had fallen victim. For Lyra, it seemed her whole damned head had suffered the damage.

The man in front of her was not tame in the least. He was nothing short of a god. The kind of chiseled jaw you read about, dark brown hair that somehow screamed for a girl to paw at it, and five o'clock shadow to die for. That was to say nothing of his body. He was currently kneeling before her girls.

"Are you a real superhero?" Alyssa was asking. Lyra had noticed the shirt the man was wearing as well, though likely not for the same reasons her daughter had.

Lyra was looking at the way it pulled taught over broad muscled shoulders and a chest that made her breath catch. Alyssa was likely referring to the Captain America logo on the front of it.

The man raised soul-searing eyes and winked at Lyra before lowering his voice to answer Alyssa with a conspirator's whisper. "I'm not supposed to give away my secret identity. That's lesson number one of being a good superhero." He assumed a more bashful look. "Honestly, though, I'm still working on my superhero identity. I'm a little new at it and I haven't ironed out all the kinks."

Kink. Lyra shook her head at her reaction to the man. This was *not* at all like her. Then again, it wasn't like she dated a whole lot. Being a single mom of four-year-old twins could take a toll on a girl's social life. She stepped closer and put her hand on Alyssa's shoulder. Not that it would slow down her little girl's questions. Alyssa wasn't shy about going after what she wanted, and answers were no exception. Prentiss, on the other hand, was happy to stand silently by and listen as Alyssa did all the work.

Lyra couldn't help but notice she was listening avidly, though. She was as interested in the answers as Alyssa was.

"Can you introduce us to Wonder Woman?"

The man let out a big laugh at Alyssa's question and tugged at one of the twisty pigtails framing her face. "Sorry. Like I said, I'm new at this. I have no clout with Wonder Woman yet. She's a little high up in the ranks, you know?"

He stood to his full height and thrust a hand toward Lyra. "I'm Luke Reynolds. I'll be your super for the next month."

Lyra took his hand and mentally swatted at the swoon happening in her head as his warm hand engulfed hers. She could practically hear her girlfriends giggling and telling her to enjoy the moment.

She shook the voices right out of her head and smiled. "What happened to Kyle?" Kyle was the young doctorate student who normally served, for better or worse, as the building's super.

Alyssa answered for him, so they must have already covered this territory. Leave it to Alyssa to challenge anyone new in the building. "He's counting testicles."

Lyra could feel the heat race to her face as her eyes shot to the man in front of her, but her new super took it in stride. He looked down at Alyssa, the edges of his lips twitching as a smile tried to break free. "Tentacles. He's counting tentacles." Now he turned to Lyra. "Kyle is going to be on board a marine biology vessel tracking a mutation in the number of legs in some kind of octopus for the next month. From what I'm told, it's a dream internship for someone in his field."

"Ah." Lyra nodded.

Kyle was a nice enough kid, but he wasn't the greatest super in the world. He tried, but his skill level at fixing things left something to be desired. She could put up with looking at this guy for the next month for sure, and who knew, maybe he'd turn out to be good at fixing things as a bonus.

Her friends' voices were back in her head with all kinds of comments about fixing things, complete with Joey Tribbiani-style grins and nods.

"Anyway, you're stuck with me." Luke smiled again and damn if her panties didn't start trying to wriggle right off. This had to end. Had to.

Prentiss tugged on her sleeve, drawing Lyra's attention back to the girls.

"Uncle Billy says I can take apart his old clock." Prentiss pulled a digital alarm clock from her backpack and looked up at Lyra patiently, wide brown eyes waiting.

"Oh goodie." Lyra pulled her keys from her bag and moved toward their door, marked 1 B. "Sorry," she said over her shoulder to her new across-the-hall neighbor and temporary eye candy, "apparently, we've got technology to reverse engineer."

Alyssa rolled her eyes. Unlike her twin, she was much more into fashion than engineering. "I have to plan our outfits for tomorrow." She said this to Luke as though he should understand it, and he nodded with equal solemnity, not missing a beat.

Lyra wondered if he had kids.

"Hey, let me know if you come up with any ideas on that superhero identity thing. I can use all the help I can get." His expression was completely serious and Lyra was now sure he must have kids, or maybe nieces and nephews at the very least. Some small part of her hoped it was nieces and nephews and not a wife and kids.

It sucked when he caught her looking for a ring on his

finger a heartbeat later. She blushed and turned away. "Okay, girls, let's get out of Luke's hair."

And get him out of mommy's head. She must be tired. The man was criminally good looking, but still, he shouldn't be such a distraction. She had dinner to prep and lunch boxes to wash and reload for the morning. She didn't have time to fantasize about things like the Incredible Hunk or Handsome Man or any number of just-right superhero names she could come up with for her new neighbor.

CHAPTER THREE

Luke stared at the information the commander had sent him. For the most part, he was on his own on this op, but the commander was funneling as much information as he could Luke's way. It wasn't much, but they were working with the guy who'd tipped them off to the online group. Privacy and peer pressure were giving the people in the group a false sense of security. From what Luke could gather, Brain Trust —as the group was called—was as closed mouthed as Fight Club. First rule of Fight Club and all that. Luckily for them, one guy had finally seen the potential for harm in the online group and had done the right thing. He'd alerted someone who alerted someone, who got word to the right people. They'd brought in the commander to take care of it.

It was a damned good thing, too. The online room was invite only, but it contained people working in finance, chemical research labs, companies with defense contracts, and more. All were young and up and coming people whose intelligence level far surpassed their street smarts. In many cases, they were somewhere on the genius scale. They reminded Luke of a guy he'd gone to school with. The kid had easily been the smartest guy in their class, but he'd been insanely naïve when it came to anything requiring the least bit of common sense. Luke remembered taking driver's ed with the kid and being in the back seat when it was brainiac's turn to drive. Saying it was scary was putting it mildly. It was a little like putting a robot behind the wheel. One who couldn't calculate anything other than something that had been preprogrammed into his head. And, apparently, driving wasn't in his programming.

They'd driven up onto several people's lawns because the kid was incapable of determining how far to turn the wheel. He couldn't seem to move the vehicle enough to point it onto the road without going over the middle line and across to the lawn on the opposite side of the road.

A lot of the people in Brain Trust seemed to be like that. Highly advanced in some ways, hopelessly ignorant in others. Within Brain Trust, they played what they thought were role playing war games. Things like, how would you get ahold of this or how would you hack that? How would you break chemical A out of plant B? What would it take to sabotage transportation from this area to that area at such and such time.

Some of it was theoretical. Someone would pose a question like, *what kind of damage could you do with* CRISPR? The acronym stood for clustered regularly interspaced short palindromic repeats, and as Luke understood it, the technology had to do with bacterial defense systems. When you put a bunch of geeks into a virtual room and asked them to play around with CRISPR scenarios, the shit you get is a whole lot of scary. New levels of scary. They came up with ways to attack a single race of people, provided you could get enough information about that race's genome.

Naturally, they also came up with a few ways to get their hands on that genomic data. In fact, they'd come up with several ways to get their hands on masses and masses of genomic data, in addition to things like data from those health trackers everyone was into wearing nowadays. The ones that counted your steps and activity. They had ideas for things you could do with that data, as well. None of it set Luke's mind at ease.

If you looked through the history of the group, you would see gradually more and more information being shared. Most of the time, the person leaking the intel would say "hypothetically this" and "hypothetically that," but the commander's people had checked much of it. These people were releasing actionable information in some pretty scary industries. As more and more of them shared information, there seemed to be a collective sense that they could do so without risk. The members seemed to want to one-up one another with what kind of information they could provide.

Luke had poured through almost all of the chatter they'd been able to access, going back months, and he was sure there were a few moles in the group. Identities that had been set up by the organizers purely to goad others into talking about things they shouldn't talk about.

The most secure course of action would be to go in and shut it all down. They could go to the companies involved and help them close loopholes and weaknesses that had been identified. Shoring up reserves and getting the people involved out of positions where they had access to any kind of sensitive information. They would do that, eventually. But first, they needed Luke to track the person or people behind it. If he didn't, they would simply close shop and start up somewhere else.

Luke had started by cataloguing who he thought each

actor was. He was sure he'd identified at least five fake profiles based on their activity. The fake profiles seemed to offer less in terms of their own information or strategies, choosing instead to egg on or encourage others. In fact, that seemed to be the main purpose of the accounts he'd flagged.

Three of them were the bold type who agitated others in the group on. The other two had been harder for him to spot. They weren't leaders. They were quiet and reserved, but every so often, they would pipe up with a piece of supposed intel just at the right moment in the game to push someone else into revealing something. The pattern was only noticeable when you looked at things in the group from a big picture scenario—something Luke happened to excel in from his days as a SEAL.

He suspected there were really one or two actors behind the false identities.

The one thing they knew for sure was that the person behind the private chat room was living in the apartment across the hall from him right now. Since he was guessing it wasn't one of the cute twins with the big brown eyes he'd just met, that left the other occupant.

Somehow, he didn't want to believe the chestnut-haired woman with the intense eyes was behind it, but he also knew things could get tight for a single mom. From the information he'd been given, Lyra Hill had been widowed before her girls were born. She worked for a company that made customized iPhone apps for small businesses and had no criminal history.

There'd been an easy smile on her face and the dusting of freckles across pale peach-toned skin said *girl next door* not *cybercriminal*. He'd felt bad about the recording device hidden in the button of his Henley. At least it wasn't being transmitted to a backup team somewhere. He was simply downloading and storing the recordings for his own use and to have a record when and if they needed to justify this op.

Still, he felt awful for some reason. Maybe it was because she and her daughters were the picture of a loving mom and kids. The girls shared her eyes. Their skin might be mocha brown, but their cheeks had the same smattering of freckles across the bridge of their noses. There was no mistaking the relationship, and there'd been no mistaking the girls had been loved by their mom. Their interactions had screamed of it.

One had been outgoing and friendly, with no reservations. The other didn't exactly appear shy, so much as she seemed happy to remain quiet and observe the world. Then again, her sister had talked enough for the both of them. Maybe she simply had no need to talk much.

Luke shook his head at himself as he closed out his computer programs and began to shut down his computer. He had clearly lost his edge. As an operative years before, he'd never have been so distracted by the woman and her children. His mind would have been on one thing and one thing only. The job. There was no doubt he'd lost something of the focus and intensity he'd once had. But again, something needled at his brain. Something that said the woman he'd met an hour earlier wasn't the person behind the online group.

The secure phone he'd been given by the commander beeped an incoming text alert.

They're moving on setting up auction. Working on getting you in as a bidder.

Luke closed the screen and put the phone back in the drawer to his left. He had a feeling the commander was hoping to take down a few of the bidders with this job, as well. Now that he'd seen the kind of information they were looking to sell, Luke couldn't blame him. This type of information would be attractive to terrorist groups, cartels, and your general extremist groups of all shapes and sizes.

If they kept the group in play, they could gather a lot of intel before shutting it down. He only hoped the gamble was worth it. Some of the information being shared in that group could lead to a hell of a lot of lives lost.

He had just pulled up one of the screens he used for running background checks to look into the building's other residents when his phone rang. This time, it was his personal phone.

"'Lo?" He clicked through computer screens, then added the name of the guy living next to Lyra in 1D. It didn't take a genius to see the guy was a complete creep. In fact, when he'd met Aiden James in the hall earlier, the asshole had told him all about Lyra, complete with lewd gestures and the kind of grin he thought would get Luke to join in on the trash talk. *Asshole.*

"Hey, I'm at your place. Where the hell are you?" His brother's message came through loud and clear. He'd expected Luke to be sitting and waiting for him as though he had no life.

He didn't, really, now that Naomi was off to school, but still. It wasn't like Zach needed to stress that fact to him. Besides, Luke *did* get out. He played on a local baseball team every Saturday morning, and usually went for beers with the guys once or twice a week. Okay, maybe once or twice a month.

"I'm not there." He clicked through a few more screens, honing in on Aiden James' state criminal record. It was scant, but it was more than Lyra's. Nothing related to cyber-crimes. One thing Luke did in his job was help people interpret criminal records. It could often be hard to decipher whether a charge on a record was for an arrest that was later withdrawn or dismissed, or if a person had been tried and convicted of the crime. Aiden had been arrested but not tried for malicious destruction of property and second degree assault when he was nineteen. The case was dismissed without going to trial. Could be a bar fight or something along those lines where arrests were made on scene only to have the charges dropped once the people involved agreed to make reparations.

"I know you're not here. I just told you that."

Luke laughed. It was just like Zach to say something like that. It wasn't going to change the fact that Luke wasn't at his place.

"Hey." Zach's voice came through loud and clear, his annoyance along with it.

"Sorry. Just running a background check." Luke took a minute to look and see that there was no federal record for James before turning away from the screen. "I'm not home. I'm staying at a friend's place for awhile."

"Why would you do that?"

"Doing him a favor. He's the super at an apartment building nearby. Got a great gig on some boat for a month, so I said I'd stay here for him." In reality, the commander had arranged for the super to get the job on the boat, knowing it would be something he would jump at since he was in a marine biology program at school and the internship would be a huge boost to his resume. As far as the real super knew, the building manager was sending a temporary super to stay in his place and he was damned lucky they were being so accommodating for him.

"Uh huh. Does this have something to do with the job you told me about?" Zach's tone told Luke he didn't buy it. Apparently, he wasn't as easy to fool as a hungry student eager to get on board a boat and count tentacles. Or testicles. Luke chuckled.

"What's funny?" Zach asked.

"Nothing. Sorry. It's just something I'm taking care of for a friend. If you're that worried about me, I can send you the address. You can come over and check on me. Tuck me in."

Zach snorted. "I was thinking we could grab a beer, watch the game. But if you're ready for bed, old man . . ."

Luke felt a grin split his face. He'd never tell anyone, but he was glad Zach had settled back here after leaving the military. He was glad they'd stayed close, that he'd had Zach around to help him raise Naomi. His thoughts wandered for a split second to the woman across the hall, wondering if Lyra's family was close and helped her with the girls. He shoved the thoughts away. "I'll text you the address. Bring the beer."

CHAPTER FOUR

"Sorry!" Lyra pulled the laundry basket onto her hip and threw an apologetic look at her friends. Savannah and Tracy both knew what it was like to have your hands full with laundry. Savanah had three kids under seven and Tracy had two preteens. "I'm so sorry. Give me two seconds to throw this laundry in and then we can go."

She grabbed her purse with her free hand and tried to dig for the keys one-handed.

"Give me that." Savannah took the laundry basket.

Tracy lifted a pair of Prentiss's jeans from the pile and laughed as the three of them started down the staircase to the basement laundry room. She held up the spot on the knee where Lyra had stitched a ladybug over a hole. "If only I could figure out how to make a Justin Bieber knee patch, I might be able to get away with this on my girls' clothes."

Tracy's girls had entered the dreaded pre-teen years, something Lyra only thought of with shivers.

Their laughter died when they entered the laundry room.

A low muffled curse floated out from under the large utility sink across the room. That wasn't what stopped the women in their tracks, though. It was the jean clad legs sticking out. Lyra's eyes began at the well-worn boots and traveled the length of the legs. Legs that filled out the jeans a little too damned nicely. Hips that made her blush thinking about . . .

Damn, she needed to stop.

"Hi there." Savannah's tone dripped with amusement.

Luke grunted as he pushed out from under the sink and took in the audience he'd collected. He sat casually, long arms leaning on his knees as he leaned back. When he got to Lyra's face, he smiled.

"Hey, Lyra. Sorry, I'm just wrestling with the sink. It's got a leak."

Lyra laughed. "Oh, I know. I told Kyle about that leak two weeks ago. He tried repairing it with some plumber's tape, but that lasted about a day."

He grinned. "It seems he tried some kind of glue after that." He held up a saws-all. "I'm going to have to cut through the pipes and replace them to undo the damage he did."

Lyra shook her head. "He's a nice guy, but there are some things he needs to learn not to do on his own."

Tracy cleared her throat.

"Oh, sorry! These are my friends, Tracy Burrows and Savannah Williams." When Lyra glanced in the direction of her friends, she tossed in a look that said *don't embarrass me in front of this man.* The women were all innocence and raised brows. "Tracy, Savannah, this is my temporary super, Luke Reynolds."

Luke stood and wiped his hands on a rag before shaking hands with both women. Neither woman heeded Lyra's glare. Savannah fanned herself theatrically and Tracy absolutely leered.

"Wow," Savannah said, her hand not ceasing its flapping. "Lyra didn't mention this *development* to us."

Luke grinned and glanced Lyra's way, seemingly not bothered by the attention or the fact Lyra's face was likely bright red now. At least, it felt bright red to her, if that was possible.

"Pleasure to meet you." His tone said he was sincere and Lyra just hoped Savannah and Tracy didn't embarrass her any further.

The thought was fleeting and hopeless, apparently.

Tracy tossed a cheeky grin Lyra's way before leaning toward Luke. "Just how long is temporary?"

"A month."

"A lot could happen in a month." Savannah's expression filled in the rest of her innuendo and Lyra didn't waste any time shoving her friends past Luke and over to where the two washers and dryers sat.

"Enough, you two. Luke has work to do and we have to get to lunch. My lunch break doesn't last forever." Lyra worked from home most days, but she still had to keep a regular schedule to communicate with clients and the others in her office. She also had to finish her workday in time so she could get the girls. She didn't have the luxury of stretching out her lunch break and adding the time to the end of the day.

At least the women waited until they left the building minutes later to grill her. Luke had smiled and waved at them all on the way out the door, and Lyra had to admit, it had brought a stupid flip flop response to her stomach. She wasn't about to admit that to anyone other than herself, though.

"You didn't feel the need to tell us about the Baldwin?" Tracy asked as the women climbed into her Mazda.

"The Baldwin?" Lyra asked, with a small shake of her head.

Tracy shrugged a shoulder. "The hot guy—as in, as hot as a Baldwin brother?"

Lyra laughed. "Where did you come up with that?"

Another shrug from Tracy, this one with a haughty sniff. "I know things."

Savannah leaned over the front seat. "I'm pretty sure no one says that anymore, but never mind what you call him. From my calculations, if he's taking over for the super for a month, that puts him in the apartment across the hall from you for that month. That's some seriously advantageous geography."

Tracy quickly nodded her agreement. "That's a lot of chances for accidental run-ins."

"And what a body to run into." Savannah wasn't going to stop, despite the looks Lyra was giving them both.

They had a point. The man was fun to fantasize about.

Savannah's next words had Lyra's mind screeching to a halt. "He likes you, too. You should take advantage of the access this month and have a fling. You need it."

"What are you talking about? You're crazy!"

Savannah shook her head while Tracy laughed. "You can look at me like that all you want, Lyra. It's not going to change facts. That man was eying you like you were dessert. Or a side of beef, or whatever it is that men think about when they think of a hot woman. Personally, I think of chocolate when I think of a hot man. Licking melted chocolate off those muscles would sure be worth my time."

"You just compared me to a side of beef. Thanks for that." The words were softened with the smile on Lyra's face and the laughter in her voice. Ten minutes with her friends and she was relaxed and happy. Life couldn't get any better than that.

Not true. Ten minutes with Luke . . .

"You're welcome." Savannah sat back in her seat. "And I'm not crazy. That man wants you. Time to let yourself live a little and run with it. What's the worst that could happen?"

Lyra didn't answer. She could think of a lot of things that could happen. Plenty, in fact.

Luke might be nice to look at, but she wasn't about to let anything or anyone derail her plans right now. She had too much riding on things she'd lined up. Keeping her eye on the ball right now could mean the difference between getting her girls into a house she owned with a yard of their own instead of the apartment building. It could mean the difference between being able to start a savings fund for them to go to college someday and leaving them on their own to try to support any aspirations or goals they had.

She wasn't about to put any of that at risk for a man. No matter how many muscles he sported or smiles he threw her way. No ma'am.

CHAPTER FIVE

Luke closed the phone and tucked it back into its drawer, turning the lock. He didn't want to know where the commander had gotten him the budget he'd just been quoted. Shoot, for all he knew, it was funny money, appearing only in a bank account made to look like it was being transferred to the bad guys. He had a feeling not, though. For one thing, he didn't think even the federal government could manipulate the banking system that way. For another, he had a feeling the commander had been given whatever funds he needed to run the ops he was currently overseeing. Likely, the budgets were off the grid and not available to any oversight committee review. All the more reason for Luke not to ask any damned questions.

He was okay with that. What he wasn't okay with was what he just had to do to keep his fake identity in the bidding for the Brain Trust. There was no swallowing back the acid clawing at his throat right now.

The group behind the Brain Trust was moving forward

with its plans for an auction, and they were moving forward in stages. Stage one was a buy-in bid for the chance to bid on the next round. The payoff? Not only would you get to the next round, you'd gain access to their proof-of-product. The leaders of the group would be pulling some kind of one-off crime. Something large enough to prove to the bidders that they had a package of information worth buying.

Luke just hoped like hell that didn't mean taking lives. He'd been poking around in the chat room long enough to know it could mean something as big as taking down a plane or releasing a chemical compound that could kill hundreds, if not thousands. He was praying they'd choose something more discreet. In fact, that's what he was banking on. He'd battled with his own conscience and argued with the commander, but the end analysis led them both to the same conclusion. It was simply a risk they had to take.

If they wanted to actually put an end to this for good, to get all the players involved and take down some of their buyers in the process, he'd need to do this. He rubbed a hand over his chest. It sure as hell didn't make this part of it any easier. Working undercover always held an element of unease. You had to do what you were hardwired not to. SEALs, cops, agents—most went into the job because of an innate drive to seek justice. To defend the vulnerable, to do right no matter the cost. So, shoving aside that drive for the greater good came at a hard price.

He'd watched Zach do this back when Zach was working vice, running undercover drug deals. He had seen the wear on his brother as time went on. He was sure Zach still held some scars from that time. Hell, Zach probably held a lot of scars from his time as a cop. He was a detective now in major crimes. What he saw from day-to-day had to be bad.

Maybe he could ask Zach how he managed to keep going day after day with this feeling in his gut.

For now, he shoved aside the ball of heartburn simmering there and focused on day-to-day routines to try to erase the guilt.

Luke headed for his kitchen to grab the laundry basket he'd tossed on his counter earlier, when his phone rang. The incoming FaceTime call from Naomi was enough to wash the grim thoughts swamping his mind. She could always bring a smile to his face.

"Hey, Naomi." He held the phone up, soaking in the sight of her. She was sitting on a bench in what looked like the central area on her campus. He could see the quad behind her, students crossing the grass in groups or pairs. "Everything all right?"

She shook her head but there was a grin softening her look. "I'm fine. I'm *always* fine." She had told Luke and Zach over and over they didn't need to worry about her so much. The lesson never took, and he doubted it ever would. She was his world.

"How's school?" He grabbed the handle of the laundry basket and headed out into the hall with her still on screen as she told him about classes. He liked listening to her tell him about her world. It made him feel like she was still close by.

The unmistakable sound of Lyra's girl racing down the hall reached his ears and he had to shove aside guilt again. Naomi had bought his line about helping a friend out by staying at his place for a month more easily than Zach, but he hated the fact he was going to have to introduce her to the girls and Lyra.

Bad enough he was leading Lyra on to trap her into implicating herself.

There was a time he wouldn't have cared. He had a job to do and that job required him to pretend to be someone he wasn't. Completing his mission would save untold numbers of people, so he'd do it without a moment's hesitation or remorse. It's part of what made a SEAL a SEAL. The willingness to run hell-bent and flat-out toward danger and stick your life in front of another's, even if that person was a stranger.

So, he hated that he now had the urge to hang up on Naomi so she wouldn't meet the girls. So she wouldn't ask later what had happened to Lyra and if he ever saw her or her twins anymore. Naomi would ask. She was that type of person. She cared about others and thought about strangers in ways others might not.

The urge to hang up came too late. Already Naomi was smiling and asking who was making all the noise. Luke knelt to meet the girls at their level. Rather than hitting the camera icon that would turn his camera toward the girls and allow Naomi to see what he was seeing, he turned the phone so Prentiss and Alyssa could see Naomi.

As he'd come to expect in the last few days, Alyssa and Prentiss were dressed alike, but there were distinct differences to their appearance. Alyssa wore her hair in neat pigtails, a sausage curl coming out on either side of her head, purple bow at the base of each. The bows matched her dress, complete with frills and not a spot of her lunch or dirt or whatever else a child of her age would run into throughout the day marking it.

Prentiss, on the other hand, sported the same dress and pigtails, but one bow had come undone, the pigtails loose and disheveled rather than neatly primped. There was a spot of what he would swear was grease from a car or other engine on her dress and the knees of her leggings showed the evidence of having knelt in dirt at some point in the day.

He'd discovered Alyssa was the one who dressed them in matching outfits each day. According to Lyra, Alyssa was into fashion and enjoyed planning their outfits. Prentiss didn't mind dressing in whatever Alyssa chose for her, so, Lyra had told him with a shrug, that's the way they arranged things.

Luke turned the phone to face the girls. "Naomi, meet Prentiss and Alyssa. Girls, this is my niece, Naomi."

"She's an all-grown girl." Alyssa's statement was matter-of-fact.

Luke put on a big sigh as Lyra walked up to join them. "She is an all-grown girl. I had to let her go to college this year. Can you believe she picked a school that's a four-hour drive from here?"

"I'm never moving out. I'm going to live with my mom forever," Prentiss said, bringing a laugh from all the adults, including Naomi.

"Not me," said Alyssa, a lift to her chin. "I'm getting my own place with a walk-in closet."

Prentiss scowled and Luke had a feeling she was trying to work out in her head how she could live with her mom but also go with Alyssa. Little did they know they'd both be clamoring to get out by the time they were old enough to move away. Not that Lyra didn't seem like a great mom. She did. But, it was a given all teenagers would want to spread their wings and fly.

"It's nice to meet you girls," Naomi said on the screen and before he knew it, she and the girls were chatting away while he was nothing more than their phone holder. Alyssa was telling Naomi about their birthday party their mom was planning. Apparently, she was putting together a new outfit for them that was, as she put it, "more for big girls than little girls" since they'd be turning five. Five was apparently some cut-off for little girlhood in her head.

"Laundry?" Lyra mouthed with a nod to his basket.

"Yup. Almost out of BDUs."

She shot him a questioning look and he tugged at his pants. "Cargo pants." Not exactly, but close enough for a civilian. He'd never given up the large pockets and handy loops of a good pair of Battle Dress Uniform pants despite being out of the service for years.

She nodded and whispered over the chatter of the girls. "You're in the military?"

He offered a head shake. "Was. Retired."

She nodded and looked at the time on her phone screen. "Hey girls, we have to run. Say goodbye to Luke and Naomi."

The girls gave a quick wave with varying versions of goodbye coming from both sides of the conversation and took off down the hall.

"It was nice meeting you, Naomi," Lyra called out as she followed the twins.

Luke would have turned to watch her go, were it not for Naomi still being on the phone. Instead he made his way down the hall toward the laundry room, knowing full well, Naomi would grill him if she sniffed so much as a hint of extra attention toward Lyra. She was dead set on him meeting someone to date now that she was "out of his hair," her words not his.

"She's pretty."

Luke looked at Naomi and shook his head. "You barely

saw her." His groin was wholeheartedly agreeing with her—and then some—but he wouldn't let on.

Her laughter said she wasn't buying it. "And her girls are adorable."

The statement gave him an idea for another defense and he snatched at it as he settled the phone against his detergent bottle on the table in the laundry room and set about loading the washing machine.

"What makes you think she's single? You saw her kids." He knew Lyra was single, but he didn't see any reason to confirm or deny that with Naomi.

She made the kind of dismissive sound she'd perfected with him. "I can tell these things. Besides, there isn't a ring on her finger."

How had she seen that? She might be right, but he felt the need to keep going. "Not every woman wears one."

"Admit it. She's single." A pair of legs came up behind the bench Naomi sat on and she turned to talk to someone else for a minute. It was clear she was about to end the call. He'd been lucky to have her this long. Naomi seemed to be settling into campus life just fine. A pang of something hit him. Jealousy, maybe? Not for the experience she was having, but for the fact he wasn't there with her. Zach was right. He'd turned into a middle-aged housewife experiencing empty-nest syndrome. It was pretty sad.

"Sorry, Uncle Luke. I have to run to a study group." She smiled and gave him one of the lines from their Winnie the Pooh Song. "You'd be surprised there's so much to be done."

He laughed. "Honey jars on noses, huh?"

"I wish. It turns out, statistics is harder than I thought, but the study group is helping. I'll talk to you soon." A few kissing sounds through the phone and she was gone.

Fuck, he was a sad sap. He shoved clothes into the

machine harder and lifted the phone, texting his brother. He needed to get out of here tonight. With any luck, Zach could meet him for a beer and they could do manly shit like drink, watch a ball game, and limit all communication to grunts. That might give him his balls back.

CHAPTER SIX

Lyra attempted to bury all thoughts of the sexy super as she entered the building. She'd gotten Prentiss and Alyssa to school as close to eight thirty as possible. All right, it had been eight forty, but she rarely made the eight to eight thirty window for drop off. Who could blame her? With Alyssa chattering away and Prentiss working on deciphering some engineering problem that would be advanced for a ten-year-old, much less her four years, the mornings didn't exactly move along like one of Prentiss's clocks.

And Lyra was no morning person. She thrived on working late into the night. Not something that was conducive to raising twins on your own.

This morning, the girls had run their suggested names for Luke's superhero identity past her. She had managed to keep a straight face to Muscle Man, but had a harder time with Rough Tough Guy and Truck Man. The girls had been solemn-faced as they explained the name was supposed to be based on what the person was. They'd taken that literally.

"I'm a truck?" Luke had looked truly puzzled, and she had to admit, that was cute as sin. The way he was with her girls was more than a little endearing, but it was also a temptation she didn't need. She didn't need to start fantasizing about a father for the girls.

"No, silly." This came from Prentiss, which surprised Lyra. She seemed to like talking to Luke. She wasn't afraid to push her way into a conversation, even if it was being dominated by Alyssa, so long as Luke was involved. "You're as big as a truck. But Big-as-a-Truck Man is a mouthful." This last was accompanied by an eye roll that was beyond adorable, but Prentiss wouldn't appreciate hearing that, so Lyra bit down on her lip.

Prentiss told him not to worry. That they were just "pot boiling." Lyra had corrected that to "spit balling" and Prentiss promised they'd get back to him when they had more.

Luke had done that thing where he tilted his head back and laughed, and Lyra couldn't help but smile at the memory. She slid her key in her lock now, then jumped a mile at the sound of a deep, smooth voice behind her. No part of her pounding heart processed it was Luke and that the words he'd uttered were offering her coffee—otherwise known in her world as Sustenance of the Gods—as she spun.

The look he gave her was one of wry amusement. "Jumpy much?"

"You scared the crap out of me. I didn't even hear your door open."

He grinned and looked back at the offending door before turning back to her with a lazy shrug. "It did." He raised his mug. "Coffee?"

Lyra glanced at her phone screen, hedging. "I need to get started on work. I'm running late."

He turned and walked into his place, waving her in with one hand. "You can take it with you and return the mug later."

She padded after him and glanced around at the neat room. It was nothing like it had been just a week before. Not that she went into her superintendent's apartment. Living across the hall, though, she had easily seen the sloppy quarters of the permanent tenant. Luke, on the other hand, had the place scrubbed and tucked away, or however it was that you'd say that in the military. She was sure there must be a term for it.

The furniture and stuff was all the same, of course. But he'd put things away and had only the bare minimum of things around on shelves and desk or table space. A slim laptop sat with its top shut on the built-in desk in the corner and the kitchen table held only a roll of paper towels in its center.

"What is it?" Luke asked following her gaze around the room as he poured her coffee.

"It's just so much neater than Kyle kept it."

"I like things neat." He held up the mug. "Cream or sugar?"

She scowled at him. "Don't you dare taint its efficacy with crap like that."

That brought a chuckle from him and she made a mental note not to make him laugh or smile. The man was gorgeous without that, but add in the lightness of a laugh and his face did things it shouldn't be allowed to do.

"Yes, ma'am."

She damned near spilled the liquid as he handed it to her. There was a silken tone to his voice and she'd swear he'd just taken it an octave lower, the hint of a promise in his response.

Lyra sucked in a deep breath and turned to the door. She needed to get the hell out before it was too late. "Thank you," she said as she all but bolted.

"So, what do you do?"

Really? He was really making small talk as she was trying to run for the door. She turned back, keeping half her traitorous body in the doorway. "I, uh, I work for a company that designs phone apps and computer software specific to client needs and marketplace demands."

He laughed, and for some reason her mind spiraled off into a crazed fantasy that involved a lot of licking and nibbling. Where the hell had that come from?

"You sound like a walking marketing brochure." His tone was light and easy as he lifted his cup to his mouth, but his eyes held her, pinned in place.

She shrugged. "Sorry. My boss has drilled that one into all of us. I think he took a course on elevator pitches and he sort of locked in on the concept."

"It isn't a bad one."

As he relaxed, leaning a hip on the couch that took up a large portion of the small living space, she relaxed as well. "No, it's really not. I've just worked for this company a little too long, I guess."

That was putting it mildly. She'd put up with a boss who knew far less than anyone working for him, but somehow he'd managed to start his company and keep it running well enough to get away with a surprising level of ignorance about their work. She knew he had his father's money backing him and she'd never quite been able to muster up respect for him.

"You don't like it?" She got the sense he truly cared about the response and she felt a little bad for trying to run out with his coffee without even an attempt at conversation.

"I like the work, just not working for someone else. I won't be there much longer, though. If I hang in another month or so, I'll be golden." She glanced at her phone as an incoming text sounded. "Speaking of working for someone else, I've got to run. Thank you for the coffee," she said and turned to flee, guilt be damned.

The coffee was really entirely too good, and she didn't actually have to start work just yet. Truth be told, the text she'd gotten was from Tracy asking if she'd had any more contact with her sexy neighbor.

Since she'd found herself ready to pour out her plans for economic independence to her new neighbor, she'd decided to take advantage of the excuse to clear out of there. The last thing she needed was to be sucked into a guy who somehow made idle chit chat over coffee feel like the hottest date she'd had in a damned long time.

Luke watched Lyra as she shut the door between them. He hated that she'd lit up when she talked about being able to leave her job soon. He'd been thinking he could clear her and start working on finding the real person behind the online group, but the light in her eyes when she talked about being able to leave her current job needled at him. Could she really be the one behind this group?

She sure as hell had the technical know-how to get the job done, didn't she? She worked with computers. She built apps. It would be a piece of cake for her to set up a chat room like this one, and her innocent single mom thing would lure people in. Anyone would feel comfortable talking to her.

His mind went to the people in the chat room, in particular the ones he'd pegged as false identities that might really be their perpetrators. None had used her exact profile of a single mom of two young girls, but one talked about working for a small company in computers, and mentioned being a mom at one point. No real specifics, but enough that it could be Lyra.

"Hot as fuck, isn't she?"

Luke felt a wave of anger wash over him as he turned, knowing damned well the voice would be coming from Aiden James, the asshole who lived in the last of the apartments on this floor. The one right next to Lyra and her girls. The creeper stood in his doorway in the apartment next to Lyra's one hand scratching at his exposed stomach, as he stared at the door to Lyra's apartment.

"I bet she's one of those women who'd rock your world in the bedroom, you know, man? She's all buttoned up and has the mom act going for her and shit, but fuck—" he drew out the last word as if he were picturing the act itself with Lyra. Luke had to school his expression to hide his response — "that one lets her hair down I'm telling you. I'd bet my bike on it."

Luke had to stop himself asking if it was a Schwinn or a Huffy. He knew full well from his background checks on everyone in the building the guy owned a Harley. He was also out of work and had no way to explain how he paid his rent. The apartment building wasn't high end, but it wasn't low end either. It was fairly safe and kid-friendly. Well, aside from the leering Aiden James, it was kid-friendly. If Luke ever caught the guy looking at Lyra in front of her girls like that, he'd fucking castrate the asshole.

"That sink of yours still leaking?" Luke had a list of things that had been waiting for fixing. He was using it to get inside the tenants' apartments and check things out.

"Yeah. You gonna do something about it? Kyle was useless. Took him months to get anything done."

It was a wonder Kyle still had a job.

Luke nodded and spoke, before ducking back in his apartment. "Let me get my tools."

His response to Lyra bothered him. He'd been telling himself it was only because he felt for her as a single mom. His mother had been one. Hell, he'd been a single parent himself, in a sense. But he was beginning to think his off-the-charts attraction to Lyra and the pull she seemed to have on him was more than that.

And right now, he wanted to do all he could to find someone else in this building that could be behind what was going on. Everything in him wanted to find someone else responsible. Because the idea that he'd have to take down Lyra Hill, to send the twins' mom to prison, or worse—shit, that didn't sit right at all.

CHAPTER SEVEN

The leaky sink took Luke all of five minutes to repair, but he stayed under there, messing with the pipes like it was taking him time.

"So, you lived here a long time?" He called out to Aiden, who sat in front of a computer on a desk in the living room. "It seems like a nice building."

"What? Oh, uh, yeah. It's not bad." He called in response from the other room.

Luke slid out from under the sink. "I was thinking I might lease that studio for rent up on the third floor when I'm done covering for Kyle." He walked into the living room while he wiped his hands with a rag.

Luke stopped short. The asshole was watching porn on his computer with the sound off. What kind of man watched porn with a stranger in the next room?

Aiden looked over his shoulder at Luke and laughed as he raised his hands up like he wanted to show Luke they weren't down his pants. "It ain't what it looks like. They pay me to edit this shit. I don't even get a fucking hard on watching it anymore. I've seen some crazy ass shit in this job, though, I tell you. I mean, fuck, the shit I could tell you about."

Luke bit down on the urge to spit out the word "don't" and focused on the back of Aiden's head instead of the computer screen. "Oh yeah? How'd you get into that?"

Aiden shrugged a shoulder and grunted. "My friend owns the company. He pays me to do this shit under the table, so it's a good gig. I can do it whenever I want, and really, he doesn't need me to do a lot to each video. I just clean 'em up and ship 'em out the door. The name of the game in this business is quantity not quality, man. It's not like I have to do anything fancy."

Aiden closed the screen. "See? Done. Five minutes."

Luke forced a grin. "Nice. You get paid good money for that?"

Aiden crossed his arms. "You see my bike out back? Paid for by porn." He grinned. "My buddy wants me to get into this Hentai shit, though. That's gonna take longer for the animation, but it shouldn't be bad and he's gonna have to pay me a lot more for it."

"What the hell is Hentai?" Luke really didn't want to know, but he couldn't stop himself asking the question anyway.

Aiden swiveled in his chair and picked up what looked like a comic book and tossed it to Luke.

"Oh hell." Luke tossed it back as Aiden laughed.

"I know, right? Hentai is Japanese anime porn. There are online versions where it's animated and shit. My buddy says that's all the rage right now. It even tops the searches for free porn. So, he needs me to do the animation once he gets some artists lined up to draw the shit."

Luke raised a brow. "Have fun with that."

Aiden's laugh was almost a cackle.

Luke glanced around at the computer equipment. It seemed like the guy was really into computers and Luke couldn't help but wonder what else he was using the equipment for. "All this is for editing porn?"

Aiden shrugged. "Nah. I got a few other things I do." He tipped his head toward the kitchen. "You take care of that leak?"

Luke nodded. "All set. Let me know if it gives you any more trouble." Aiden stood and walked back to the little kitchen with Luke so he could grab his tools.

Luke needed to find out what those *other things* Aiden James was doing might entail. The guy seemed to have some skill with computers and his proximity to Lyra might have made her a tempting scapegoat if he was behind the Brain Trust. He likely could have set up the servers to make it look like Lyra's computer was being used.

He almost smiled as he left the apartment. He wouldn't mind at all if it was Aiden James who was behind this. Taking down this guy would be fun. A hell of a lot more fun than finding out Lyra was behind it all.

CHAPTER EIGHT

Luke couldn't make out Lyra's thoughts as he looked at her face. She stood in her doorway looking—well, dazed was the only way to put it. Adorably dazed.

"Lunch?" She asked again.

Shit he was rusty at this. He should have listened to Naomi and dated a little more. Problem was, his only thoughts about dating in the last few years had been about Naomi's dating and how he could keep the dogs sniffing around her from acting on the teenaged fantasies he knew they were having. He knew damned well what those boys wanted from her and he'd be damned if he'd let any of them get near her in that way.

Hell, when he'd been a SEAL, it wasn't uncommon for him to sleep with a different woman whenever they had downtime between assignments. Any of the members of his team could walk into a bar, snap their fingers, and have any number of women fighting over them. It wasn't exactly dating, though. Not to mention, things had changed the second he'd become Naomi's guardian. From the moment he took that on, he'd lived like a monk. Hence, his now rusty attempts with Lyra.

And it wasn't like he really wanted to date her. She was part of the job.

He swore he heard someone cough behind him with a muffled *bullshit*, but since his brother wasn't inside his head, he guessed it was his imagination.

He was telling himself he was trying to get close to her for the sake of the case. And that was true, to a point. But hell if he wasn't also really fucking glad for the excuse.

"Yes. Lunch. As in, food. Sustenance. A break? You know. Surely, you need a break sometime during the day. I thought you could take it with me. I made lunch."

She opened her mouth, but he stopped her. "Don't say *lunch* again. Just say yes, save your work," he said with a nod toward where her computer sat on a desk behind her, "and be over in five."

He turned away and returned to his apartment, shutting the door behind him. There. Done.

Unless she didn't show up in five minutes. He shrugged, ignoring the stab of disappointment he felt at the thought. He could eat her share. He carried both plates of food over to the small table that sat between the living area and the kitchen area of the apartment and then turned back to pour two glasses of ice water. The rooms couldn't really be described as rooms. They were more like two spaces that ran into one another with the only real dividing features being the change from vinyl flooring to carpet and the table between them.

He wouldn't admit to the rush he got when he heard a little knock on his door a minute later. Not to himself and not to anyone else.

"Hey," he said as he opened to the door to find Lyra still

looking a little unsure of herself on his doorstep. "Everything's ready."

She looked a little dubiously at the table, but seemed to relax when she saw the fruit salad and tomato and grilled cheese sandwich on her plate. It wasn't fancy but it must have exceeded her expectations. "You can cook."

It wasn't the simple statement that made him laugh. It was the surprise her voice was laced with as she spoke. He pulled a chair out for her and took his own seat.

"I didn't have much choice. It was either learn to cook or Naomi and I would have been forced to live off cold cereal." Not to mention, he'd had child services checking on him to be sure he was up to the task of parenting her when he first took custody of her. It wouldn't have done to have them question anything about his abilities.

Lyra looked up. "Naomi? I thought she was your niece."

"She is. I raised her from the time she was ten." He could see the question in her eyes. He was used to it, but there was still an old ache in his gut whenever he told the story. It couldn't be helped. It was the kind of pain that would never go away, the layers of scar tissue only growing older, but no less painful. "My sister and her husband and my mom were killed in a car accident when she was ten. She survived."

"Oh," she said, her breath coming in a whoosh as she absorbed what he'd said. He knew she was likely processing the fact Naomi had been in the crash where so many had died. It was always the first thing that hit him when he thought about that day. As a mom, she would likely be thinking about that, too.

He didn't tell her, but Naomi had walked away with little more than bumps and bruises. It was a miracle he was grateful for, but one he knew had been extremely hard for

Naomi to get past. She'd watched three people she loved die that day.

Lyra looked at him with soft eyes that held a world of emotion. "I'm sorry."

The simple statement carried with it the weight of truth. It wasn't one of those empty platitudes given by so many people.

Luke nodded and took a bite of his sandwich, using the excuse of a full mouth to give himself a minute before answering. "We had a rocky start and she needed some therapy to work through the effects of being in the car at the time, but things have been good for the last few years. We're close. And my brother lives in town, too, so we have him."

They ate in silence a few minutes more before she spoke again. "You said you were in the military before. I can imagine being a single parent in the military is difficult."

"I was at the tail end of my tour when the accident happened. With the help of my CO and a few others I'd worked with over the years, I was able to leave a couple of months early. Zach still had another two years on his tour, so he stayed in."

"Is he still in the military?"

Luke was a little too fascinated with watching Lyra's mouth close over a piece of watermelon. Lord, he'd never appreciated fruit so much in his life. He wondered how she'd feel about him tracing watermelon over the curve of her neck and down to her breast, so he could lick the juice off before feasting on her.

What was wrong with him? He shifted in his seat and replayed her question in his head. She'd asked if Zach was still in the military.

"No, um." Luke cleared his throat and forced his body to cooperate. "He's a detective with the New Haven Police

Department." Ordinarily, he might not share many personal details—at least not real ones—when he was undercover like this, but he wanted to see her reaction. Not to mention, everything in him was starting to believe she wasn't the person behind the online group.

Hell, that could just be his dick talking, though. He watched her face for any sign of a reaction to the news of his brother's job, but there wasn't anything suspicious. No flicker of concern for hidden secrets. No hint of guilt or fear.

Instead, she frowned. "Do you worry about him?"

Luke tilted his head as he answered. "Some. I think it was a little hard for Naomi when he joined the force. It's why I've kept myself out of any work that puts me in the line of fire."

Until now.

"What do you do?"

"I own a business running background checks online for people." God that sounded boring as hell.

Despite that, Lyra's eyes lit. "You own your own business?"

"It lets me work from home and be around when Naomi needs me. Well, it did until she up and ran off to school on me." He tossed her a grin that said he was kidding and stood to clear their plates. "And I think it helped her to know I wasn't doing any kind of work that put me in danger at all. Like I said, she has a hard time with Zach being in the line of fire sometimes, but I think she also knows he wouldn't be happy if he wasn't doing the kind of work he does."

She brought the conversation back to his business. "So, I would have thought running background checks is all automated nowadays. You're able to make a living charging people for doing them?"

He nodded and returned to the table, this time sitting

one seat over, so he was next to her instead of across from her. "People can use other systems to run them for far less than I charge, but they don't really know how to interpret them. A report might say someone has a trespassing charge against them, but that can stem from an awful lot of things. Could be a childish prank. Could be a guy stalking someone but the cops could only get him on a trespassing charge. I help them understand what they're seeing or sometimes I dig into the details more and find out what's behind the charge. I figure out what's worth worrying about and what's not for them. I get a lot of return business from human resources departments and things because they want someone to help them through the process. Some wealthy clients who want to run everyone they date or do business with or whatever through the ringer before they trust them."

"Well, that's a hell of a way to live a life."

"I hear ya. It would suck having to be that distrustful all the time. But for the amount of money we're talking about, they have no choice. A lot of them have been burned by people in their life who aren't there for the right reasons. You can only tell so much by running a standardized report. I can tell them a little more. Help them make some decisions."

"It must have been stressful doing that when you knew you had Naomi depending on you. Starting the business, I mean." She clamped down on her lips as though she wanted to say more but didn't, and he wondered what she wanted to ask.

"It was, especially in the beginning. I didn't have a mortgage because my mom had left her house to me and Zach in the will and he let me and Naomi live there without paying him anything for his part of it. Still, paying for insurance as a self-employed person sucks, and I had to have insurance with Naomi. There are those kind of worries. I had some savings from when I was in the SEALs, so I had that to fall back on if things went downhill." He shrugged because the truth was, even with all those things in his favor, it had been a stressful time, but he hadn't had much choice. He wasn't qualified to do much in the real world.

She looked entirely too thoughtful as she nodded.

"Are you thinking of starting your own business?" He had a feeling her head was working through something and the uneasy look she gave him confirmed it. Actually, there was excitement there was well, if he looked carefully enough.

She gave a tentative nod, as though she were testing out the admission before committing to it. "Yes. I have the plan written up and I think I've accounted for everything. I've got to save a little more before I'm willing to take the plunge, though. With Prentiss and Alyssa, I can't afford to take chances."

Luke nodded and twisted the water glass he'd now drained in front of him casually, but his chest eased a fraction. No way she was planning a small business with such care if she was about to sell a truckload of classified information to some of the lowest of the low on earth. At least, it helped to tell himself that. "I can look your plan over for you, if you'd like."

She sat forward. "Really?" Then the uneasy look was back and he realized she was worried about what he might think of her plan.

"I'm sure you've covered everything. You strike me as a planner." He offered a shrug. "But if you want an extra set of eyes to see if you've missed anything, I'm happy to look at it for you."

"Thanks, I'd love that. I brought it over to a nonprofit in

town that helps small businesses and they looked over it and helped me make some adjustments to my estimates, but I'm still worried I haven't come up with everything. It'd be a huge step to leave the job I'm in right now with all the flexibility they offer me."

"Do you work from home every day?"

Soft tempting tendrils swished around her shoulders as she shook her head no. "I go in to the office at least once a week. My brother stays with the kids in the afternoons when I do that."

Luke had met her brother the other day. The girls seemed to love him, and he seemed like a nice enough guy. He also just acted like a bit of a goof.

"Your brother is able to do that?"

"Yes, he works nights at a bar, so being around the afternoon to get the girls one day a week isn't a big problem. I'm home before he has to go in. So, overall, working from home has worked out well. It was an attempt to keep my boss from showing up on my doorstep. He still shows up now and again, though."

"Your boss just shows up randomly while you're working from home? That doesn't seem like it should be included in the telemarketing package?"

Lyra laughed. "It shouldn't be. My boss is . . . Well, let's just call him a nuisance. The benefits and working from home are worth it, though."

Luke probably sounded a little too much like a protective bear as he responded. "Nuisance, how?" Yep. A lot like a black bear.

Lyra waved away his response, but her cheeks flushed. "He's harmless. He's friends with my brother and I think there was probably a time when he hoped we might date, but he knows that's not going to happen now."

"Not interested in him? Or not interested in dating?" Why did the answer matter so damned much to Luke?

Her cheeks turned even pinker as she glanced his way. "A little of both, I guess. Part of it probably had to do with the fact that he's friends with my brother. My brother might be a grown up now, or something close to it, but it's still hard to picture him and his friends as anything but a pack of kids. And honestly, they still act a lot like it. My boss owns this company, but his dad is the one that funds it. If the company doesn't do well one quarter, it's not a big deal. He can always fall back on his dad's bank account. Not exactly an appealing trait in a man."

"And the dating in general part?"

Her teeth toyed with her bottom lip. "I guess I just haven't had a whole lot of time for it. The girls keep me pretty busy, and it just hasn't been high on my priorities."

It wasn't Luke's imagination. There was a heaviness to the air between them that said they were dancing around the blatant attraction between them. "And now?"

He was teasing her a little, making her spell things out for him. He couldn't help it. Things seems to have changed between them and he didn't feel as much of an urge to hold back with her as he had before.

"I don't know, maybe if the right guy comes along I'll squeeze a date between my pedicure appointments and all my long hot baths."

Luke groaned, and he didn't try to hide it. Just the mention of her in a bath did things to him. Her eyes went wide and he grinned at her with a shrug. "Sorry. It was the bath thing."

Now she looked at him, her mouth a small oh as she processed his comment.

Before she could respond, Luke heard the distinct buzz

of his secondary cell phone. Even from within the desk drawer, he could hear it and knew it meant only one thing. New information in the case. Since they were waiting for proof of the information the auctioneers were selling off, he had a bad feeling about what he might find waiting for him on that phone.

He wanted to ignore it and keep flirting with Lyra, but that wasn't really an option. It was a cold reminder of the fact that he was here to do a job, not here to start a real relationship with the woman across the hall.

Lyra stood, glancing toward his desk. "I need to get back to work, and you probably do too, it seems."

Luke stood, as well. "Yeah, unfortunately, I do. I'm around if you need a break later, though. You know, in between those hot baths."

The flush his comment brought to her cheeks had him grinning as he shut the door behind her. It didn't last though. Not when he saw the text message.

It was a link to a news story. As he read through the details, he realized it could have been a hell of a lot worse. As it was, nobody had died. But the point had certainly been made. Whoever was behind the online auction had just proven they could redirect high-speed trains to send them barreling toward one another with hundreds of lives on board.

The sellers had even managed to make it look like a glitch was responsible, and to their credit, the train stopped moments before impact. One passenger suffered a heart attack that thankfully wasn't fatal, and others received a variety of bumps, bruises, and cuts but nothing life-threatening.

As one of those who had put forth money to make the proof of product take place, he was now in on the online bidding that would take place shortly for the entire package of information up for grabs. The knowledge didn't give him any comfort, because it also meant he was one of the people responsible for putting those passengers through what had to be one of the most frightening experiences of their lives.

CHAPTER NINE

Luke stood in his kitchen thinking he probably should have gone to the grocery store. He'd gotten tied up with running several background checks for Sutton Capital, a company his brother had connected him with that sent a lot of work his way. He'd spent an hour on the phone explaining some of the results to their human resources director.

Now he was left with either cold cereal for dinner or ordering takeout.

The dilemma was put off when he heard a knock on his door. He opened it to find Alyssa and Prentiss dressed in matching green dresses with bows on each pigtail.

"You're invited," they said, in near-unison.

Luke knelt and grinned at the girls. "Invited where?"

"To our birthday party." This came from Alyssa but Prentiss nodded as though adding her stamp of approval.

The door to their apartment opened and Lyra stepped out, digging through her purse. She smiled when she saw him. "Hi, Luke."

He wasn't given the chance to return the greeting. Alyssa spoke up before he could. "Luke is coming!"

"Coming where?" Lyra looked at him and he raised his hands to let her know he had nothing to do with the plan the girls seemed to have concocted.

"To our party!" They were in unison again.

"That's about as far as we got before you came out." Luke said. He wasn't sorry the girls had invited him.

Lyra laughed. "Tomorrow is the party with ten four and five year olds running around in a park screaming. Tonight is the friends and family pizza party. And you're very welcome to come to either of them, but for your sanity, I'd recommend coming to tonight's."

Luke schooled his features and looked at the girls. "I live for pizza." He said this with the most serious face he could muster and the girls dissolved in giggles.

He glanced up to find Lyra smiling at him. Bingo. Just what he'd been going for. Each of her smiles seemed like a prize to him. A prize he liked earning.

Alyssa and Prentiss each took a hand and pulled him out of his apartment. "Are you sure it's okay for me to crash?" Luke said to Lyra as she locked her apartment.

"Absolutely. It'll give me one more adult to talk to and I'm all about adult conversation."

Christ. He wanted to know what other adult activities she might enjoy. He was all too ready to offer up his services in any way she wanted him.

Luke pulled his keys out of his pocket and locked his own door while the girls objected to their mom's viewing them as "not adults".

The party also included Mrs. Lawson and her grandson Murphy, who had spent twenty minutes folding paper into three types of origami fish for the girls, as well as Billy and his friends. Lyra's boss, Joel, who was friends with Billy was there, as was Damon, another friend who Lyra told him completed the triangle of three who had lived together at different points on and off. While Joel seemed happy enough to spend time with the twins and answer any chattering the girls threw at him, Luke got the distinct impression he was really there to drool over Lyra.

It wasn't an impression that sat well with him.

Damon, on the other hand, did little to hide the fact he'd rather be anywhere else and was killing time until Billy could leave. He spent a lot of time on his phone and didn't seem to have any interest in talking to anyone there, no matter their age.

Tracy and Savannah were there, along with their children. Luke liked them. Both women made no effort to hide the fact that they were trying to push Luke and Lyra together. If for no other reason, he liked that about them. But they were also funny and he got the sense that they had been there for Lyra through a lot. They were close. He liked that about them, too.

The evening revolved around the girls, with cheese pizzas, hot fudge sundaes, and what seemed to be hundreds of tokens spent in the arcade at the back of the pizza place. Billy, Joel, and Damon ended up crowded around one of the race car games where they took turns in the two seats competing against each other.

Tracy and Savannah scored more points in Luke's book when they took all the kids to the arcade, leaving Lyra and Luke to "watch the table."

"So you're doing all this again tomorrow, but with more kids?"

"Yup, this is the easy one. This is a tradition Billy started a couple of years ago to get out of having to go to the kids version of the birthday party. He prefers beer and pizza and the girls think it's fun to have a grown-up party, so I never argue with it. Besides, he pays for this one." She said this with a grin and Luke laughed.

Murphy came over and interrupted. "I'm going to get Grandma home, Lyra. She's not feeling well."

Lyra looked toward the other of the two booths they'd commandeered where Mrs. Lawson sat. "Oh, I'm sorry. Is she all right?"

Luke had to admit, the woman looked pale.

Murphy nodded, but his face was set in a grim line. "She just needs to rest."

They said their goodbyes before Luke brought the conversation back around to Billy. He hated to think it, but he had to wonder if Billy was involved with the Brain Trust. He spent a lot of time at Lyra's apartment. "I guess I wouldn't have pegged the bartender as someone who wants to throw around a good chunk of money on a beer and pizza party for twin girls."

"Billy likes to spend money on anything that doesn't smack of too much responsibility. Since leaving school, he's started and stopped several businesses, and most of them failed because he doesn't like to be locked in by a business plan. His words, not mine. Billy is a very fly-by-the-seat-of-his-pants kind of guy."

"You don't strike me that way." Luke looked at her and noticed the tinge of pink that lit her cheeks. "Not that that's a bad thing. I like planning."

"Yeah, Billy and I are definitely opposites as far as that's concerned." She looked over at her brother where he was currently spinning the handle of his race car and hooting as he bested Joel on the track. "He's a good guy, he's always there for me, but he's still very much a kid at heart. I'm not sure he's going to be ready to grow up anytime soon."

"Are his friends usually in on those businesses with him? They seem pretty tight." Luke eyed the three men and had a feeling he knew why everything about the Brain Trust was leading back to Lyra. His gut clenched when he thought about someday having to reveal to Lyra just what her brother had set her up for. Looking at him, you wouldn't guess he'd do that to Lyra.

Lyra made a face. "Yeah, on occasion, Damon and Joel will run off and try something new. Joel's dad has stopped funding everything except the company I work for, since that one typically pays its own bills. Damon is a little more level-headed. After they all graduated from college, Damon went on to study psychiatry. He left that program before getting his degree, but did go and get his LCSW."

The news of Damon being a licensed clinical social worker raised another flag. Luke could see the fingerprints of someone who understood psychiatry and mental health all over the manipulations taking place in the Brain Trust. Not to mention, Damon didn't at all seem like he would want to use an LCSW for anything like its intended use.

"He's a social worker?" He asked, not quite seeing it as he looked at Damon across the room.

"No, he runs a small therapy clinic. Private practice."

The twins came rushing over with Alyssa talking a mile a minute and Prentiss nodding her agreement next to her. "We did it, Mommy. We got the mouse all the way to the top without any help from Aunt Tracy or Aunt Savvy. Nobody had to help us at all this time."

"That's fantastic, girls." Lyra pulled the girls into her lap and snuggled them. They allowed the move for a split second before they ran away.

"The mouse?" Luke asked as he watched the girls run back to an arcade game.

"You have to use your gun to pump enough air at the right target to get the mouse to go all the way up the clock. Hickory dickory dock?"

"Ah. Got it." He liked watching Lyra relax. He'd seen her laugh and smile a lot tonight, and it felt good to see.

A couple walked by the table and Luke knew they'd been sitting across the room earlier. Old habits die hard. He'd never stopped monitoring any room he was in, taking in who was where doing what. Who moved around and who stayed put. Who looked right in the space and who looked "off."

This couple was simply a young couple out for a night together. They'd eaten, and were now walking out.

The woman leaned in to the table. "Your daughters are beautiful."

Luke felt a kick in his gut at the words, but didn't have time to identify what he was feeling before the woman continued.

"Where did you get them?"

Luke tried to process the question, wondering if the woman thought maybe Lyra had run on over to a clearance sale at Macy's to pick up the twins. What on earth kind of a question was that?

Lyra didn't bat an eye, instead answering with a smile. "Right straight out of my uterus. Well, through the birth canal, so I guess I can't say *straight* out, but you get the idea."

The woman glanced back and forth at Lyra and Luke, then down to where Luke's hand rested on Lyra's. He wasn't sure when that had happened, but he was glad it had. "Oh." She seemed to struggle for a minute. "I just thought . . . "

She didn't finish the thought, but walked away with a puzzled look on her face, as though she were still trying to figure things out.

"Does that happen often?" Luke asked.

Lyra nodded. "All the time. People think they're adopted. I've even had people tell me it's so wonderful of me to have taken them. Like they don't bring more joy to my life than I could ever bring to theirs."

Luke stared at her. People walked up and asked that kind of question all the time? And she didn't flatten them?

Lyra laughed. "You get used to it and start to have fun with it. Savvy adopted Tessa. If Tessa isn't within earshot, she says she picked her up at a tag sale—best bargain she's ever gotten."

"They ask right in front of Tessa!" It wasn't a question, but she answered with raised brows and a nod anyway.

Luke felt his blood begin to simmer. "Tell me people don't ask you that in front of Prentiss and 'Lyss?" His voice was low.

"They do. I told the girls people are jealous and are hoping they can get a pair of twins of their own. They said maybe not everyone realized how rare and special twins are."

Luke let out a huff of laughter, but he was still stuck on the fact the girls had heard that.

"Hey," Lyra leaned into his line of vision and he realized he'd been glaring at some point in the distance. "If I let everything like that get to me, I'd miss the good stuff, like having those girls in my life in the first place. I can't imagine what it would have been like to lose my husband and not have any piece of him with me. They're a blessing."

The air had turned heavy and thick, and Luke realized he was now holding both her hands across the table. They weren't exactly in the most romantic of places, surrounded by the vinyl booths of the pizza place with the background ambiance of children laughing and video games buzzing.

A smile cut Luke's face and the tension. "When Naomi was little, she figured out that people sometimes questioned whether I was her dad or not if I was dragging her mid-tantrum out of a mall or a store. We had a few of those episodes in the year after the accident, when she was really struggling. One day, she decided she could use it. She starts screaming that I'm not her dad at the top of her lungs."

Lyra's eyes went wide. "She didn't."

"Oh, she did. I stopped right then and there, sat my ass down to wait for the cops to arrive."

"They didn't."

"They did. And I didn't want to be attacked by an angry mob before they got there."

Lyra now had her hand over her mouth and she seemed to be alternating between gasping in horror and laughing at the image of him sitting and waiting for the cops to arrive. "What happened?"

"Naomi thought it was a good idea for about two seconds, but when people tried to pull her away from me, she thought the better of it. Between that and being grounded for a month, she didn't try it again."

CHAPTER TEN

"What the fuck was that?" Billy paced the length of the room moving from the window to the couch and back again as he gripped the phone.

He'd been physically ill the moment he saw the newscast showing two trains barreling toward one another on tracks they weren't supposed to be on at the same time. He had recognized the scenario with the two trains as soon as he'd seen it. Thank God the person behind the setup had stopped the trains just short of a collision, but still, the passengers on them had to have been scared witless.

One man had suffered a heart attack and it was looking like he might not survive.

Billy's initial thought had been that one of the people in the Brain Trust had acted on one of the scenarios, but he dismissed that possibility right away. When they set up the Brain Trust, they'd picked their marks carefully. Everyone in the rooms had been chosen for not only their intelligence and naïveté, but also because Damon's profiling had shown they were highly unlikely to ever act on any of the information shared in the group.

That left one possible culprit behind setting those trains up to collide. And he was talking to him. "Are you fucking crazy?"

"Calm down, Billy." Damon was using the patronizing tone that always got under Billy's skin. "It was a necessary demonstration of the product. How can we expect anybody to put money out there without us proving what we have?"

"You could have killed those people. I didn't sign on for anything like that. We can go to the companies and show them what we have, or a piece of it anyway. They would have paid to see what else we had found, and to find out who gave us the information if they'd just seen a small sample of what we have. Proving it is complete bullshit. You could have killed everyone on those trains."

Silence on the other end of the line sent a chill through him, but it was the only answer he got.

"What the hell are you doing?" Billy's question was quiet, too quiet. Mostly because he had a feeling the answer wasn't something he really wanted to know. He asked the question again, louder, nonetheless. "What the hell are you doing?"

His partner's answer was frighteningly nonchalant. "I found another way for us to make more money with this. We agreed this was going to be a one-time thing. In light of that, we need to get the most we can out of it."

"What does that mean?" Every fiber of his being prickled with the uneasy knowledge that his partner's true nature—a nature he had long suspected but had been studiously ignoring—was behind this move. "What do you mean you found another way for us to make more money?"

The voice on the other end of the phone remained

bland. "Early on it made sense for us to go to the relevant companies and extort money from them in exchange for the information that we've garnered." He paused. "There are . . . other parties that will pay more for the information."

"Anyone who would pay more for this information is going to be dangerous. Very dangerous." Billy began pacing again, running a hand through his hair, leaving it standing on end.

"That's of little concern. The bidding will all be done remotely. We won't have any interaction with them, no engagement at all. Everything will be perfectly safe."

"That's not the point!" He'd now raised his voice to almost a yell. A hollow ache began in his stomach, and he was reminded how he'd foolishly once thought he'd been the one in control here. It had become evident long ago that he wasn't the one in control here anymore. But that didn't mean he needed to sit by and let this happen. He could stop this. *Had* to stop this.

He took a slow breath before speaking again. "You know perfectly well that's not the point. What people would do with this kind of information is the issue. A lot of people will die, or worse. I'm not going to be part of that."

There was only a slight pause on the other end of the phone, not enough to convince him Damon had given much thought at all to what he had said. "Well, it's not up to you, is it? If you're not happy with the situation, you walk away. But remember this, once you're out, you're out. No money, nothing to show for over a year and a half of work."

They'd spent hours every day coddling those idiots in the chat rooms. For people with such high IQs, they could really be incredibly stupid. Not to mention, putting up with the arrogance of the eggheads looking down on anyone who didn't measure up. And let's face it, that had been their profiles. The geniuses had often caught on that the fake profiles Billy and Damon were behind in the group weren't as intelligent as the others. But that arrogance had kept them in the dark about the manipulation going on.

That didn't matter. Billy would scrap all that before he'd let this information out to the kinds of people who'd pay money for it. He opened his mouth to object, but didn't have a chance to respond. The line went dead.

He stared at the phone for a minute, not all together believing what had just happened.

Fuck. He needed to find some way to fix this shit. Right now, they both had access to the information. He needed to figure out a way to close that up. To lock down access to the information until he could get this shit show back on the rails.

CHAPTER ELEVEN

Luke watched as Lyra set a bowl of pasta and a green salad on the table. The girls chattered in their chairs on either side of him, and he had to admit he found it soothing. He'd been on edge since getting news of the near train wreck. Those trains had come within feet of colliding and one man who suffered a heart attack had died later in the hospital.

Lyra's invitation to pay him back for lunch by cooking dinner had given him a welcome distraction. They'd taken a few short coffee breaks together during the week, each time sitting on either her couch or his.

There hadn't been a lot of coffee drinking happening, but something else had happened. His mind raced back to the kiss. He'd honest-to-God not known if he remembered how to kiss or not, but there was no stopping that pull when she'd been laughing and looking so damned beautiful curled up next to him.

When he'd put a hand to the back of her head and tilted it back, bringing her mouth to his, it had been like lighting a fire between them. She'd melted against him, hands coming up to his chest, stoking the flames as he delved into her mouth to taste and tease.

He shook himself out of the memory, well aware that another few seconds would leave him embarrassingly hard at the dinner table. That would go over well.

"And at the end," Alyssa was saying with an excited giggle, "Batman finally tells the Joker that he hates him." She dissolved into laughter. "Isn't it funny? Telling someone you hate them isn't supposed to make them happy. But that's what the Joker wanted all along."

Lyra grinned as she took a seat across from Luke and glanced at him. "And if you planned on seeing that movie, now you know the big ending."

"You should see it." Alyssa bounced in her seat. "You should watch it with us. We own the movie."

"He's not gonna want to watch a kids' movie, 'Lyss." Prentiss spoke with all the authority of a four-year-old going on 30. "Grown-ups don't want to watch kids' movies."

"Hey," Luke turned a raised brow to Prentiss. "*Frozen* happens to be my favorite movie."

This brought a lot of giggles from both girls and Lyra grinned at him across the table, shaking her head.

"I'm not kidding you. I know all the words to every one of the songs. It used to drive Naomi nuts when I wouldn't stop singing them around the house. And don't get her started about the carpool lane. If one of them came on while we were sitting in the carpool lane, I'd be singing at the top of my lungs while she sank down into her seat, hoping nobody would see me."

"You're fibbing!" Alyssa's accusation came with a finger point and everything.

Luke proved her wrong by tipping back his head and belting out the chorus to *Let It Go*.

He'd never been embarrassed to sing in public, but even if he had, the laughter his performance brought from Lyra was worth it. It erased any thoughts of the investigation, the narrowly avoided train wreck, and figuring out who was behind making it look like Lyra was involved.

Prentiss crinkled her brow at Luke thoughtfully. "Everyone knows that one."

Alyssa nodded in agreement with her sister.

Luke grinned at the girls, offering their mother a wink, before beginning his favorite song, *In Summer*. The song about a snowman dying to see what summer was like always made him laugh. In fact, he and Naomi both cracked up every time they heard the song or watched that part of the movie. Despite wanting to sink into a hole in the ground whenever he sang the songs publicly, she had still loved watching it and singing along with him whenever they did.

The girls dissolved into giggles, appearing suitably impressed with his depth of knowledge.

Luke finished off the song just as he always did, belting the final notes as loudly as he could. Lyra now had tears streaming down her face as she laughed at him, and he was pretty sure he never felt anything as rewarding as making her laugh like that.

"Mom," Alyssa said. "Can we watch *Frozen* after dinner with Luke?" She turned wide eyes to him. "We own that one, too."

"You do? I knew you ladies were trying to steal my heart."

Prentiss and Alyssa giggled as Lyra shot him the kind of look that asked if he really wanted to stay and watch the movie with the girls? He nodded at her. As if she could think he was faking his love of all things *Frozen*. He might be a little offended.

"With popcorn?" Prentiss asked, a slight glance shot toward her sister with the question.

"I suppose." Lyra's answer brought cheers from the girls.

"After pasta and salad." Lyra's attempt at a stern tone was unnecessary. The girls began piling pasta and salad in their mouths at a steady pace.

Lyra looked across at Luke. "I guess they know not to question your word from now on."

He'd forgotten for a minute that all this was fake. That he was getting close to Lyra for the job.

Luke kept the smile on his face but it felt as cold as if Elsa herself had conjured it there, and he was pretty sure you couldn't chisel it off with a jackhammer. Because one thing was sure, Lyra definitely couldn't take him at his word.

Lyra forced her mind to focus on getting the girls' teeth brushed and steering them into bed. It was a little hard since her mind kept going back to the man sitting on her couch. It was also hard to keep her thoughts where they needed to be where he was concerned. She should be thinking that he was too good to be true. That there *had* to be something wrong with a man who looked like him, had no problem engaging with the mindless chatter of two excited four-year-olds, and seemed to think a night of spaghetti and watching Disney movies was the height of entertainment.

He hadn't been lying about knowing every word to every song. He and the girls had even gotten Lyra to join in with him on their singing after a few rounds of simply watching and laughing. It was hard not to laugh. There was something about watching a man who looked like he could have starred in *Rambo* twirl around with her girls as they sang about building a snowman or do the funny reindeer voice for the reindeer are better than people song.

"That was fun tonight, mommy," Prentiss said, in her quieter manner than Alyssa. Alyssa had been bouncing around during the whole nighttime routine, but she'd fallen asleep as soon as her head hit the pillow. Prentiss and Lyra often had a few minutes to themselves to chat during tucking in. It was one of the parts of the routine Lyra cherished, knowing it would be all too easy for Prentiss to feel overshadowed.

"It was fun, baby." She almost said they'd need to do it again sometime the way she would for any activity they'd found that they enjoyed, but she was keenly aware that Luke was only here temporarily. Sure, he lived in New Haven, but she didn't have any reason to think they'd still see him when the month was out. She wasn't about to make promises about that to her kids. She leaned over and kissed Prentiss on the forehead, loving the soft feel of the child's skin. "Get some sleep."

Butterflies seemed to be putting on a major production of Swan Lake in her stomach as she walked back out to the living room to find Luke waiting. His head was tilted back and his eyes closed. She took a moment to watch him. He took her breath away, the same as he had the first time she'd seen him, and she found her gaze drawn to his mouth. It wasn't the first time it had distracted her. She didn't know what it was about his mouth.

It wasn't like she had a thing for lips, but his just seemed to call to her, made her itch to brush her lips against his. She glanced up to find his eyes open, watching her and the heat in them belied the smirk on his face at having caught her drooling over him.

Lyra felt her cheeks flush, but she stepped forward and sat on the couch, one seat over from him. She tucked a foot up under her and leaned her head on her hand. She couldn't think of a damned thing to say.

Luke reached out and slid his hand into her hair then let it slide through his fingers. The simple gesture seemed intimate, easy. "You must be exhausted. Those girls are a handful."

"You were the one that did all the work tonight. In fact, you guys practically put on a show for me. You'll need to watch out. Alyssa will start to put you in costumes to play your part, if you're not careful."

She meant it as a playful warning, but the level of permanency it suggested made her glance away uneasily.

Luke didn't seem to notice. He laughed it off and leaned back again. "Tell me about the girls. They seem so different at times."

"They are. Alyssa has been the leader from the get-go, but I've come to realize Prentiss is very capable of putting her foot down with her sister when she wants to. I think she simply doesn't want to."

"She likes to take things apart?"

"Mm hmm. Anything she can get her hands on. Well, anything I'll let her pull apart. I've finally gotten it through to her that she has to get permission before getting out her toolbox. She gets it from her father, I think."

"Was he an engineer or a mechanic?" Luke asked.

"No, actually. He was an investigative journalist. But, I can see the same thing in them both. There's this need to get behind things, to see what's pushing it inside, how it works. He was never satisfied with simply reporting on a story or the news as it happened. He wanted to dig deep, make connections between things no one else had been able to see. He wanted to get to the heart of things. It's the same thing with Prentiss only it takes a different form for her."

"You light up when you talk about him. You loved him a lot." Luke's words weren't a question, but she answered it as one.

"Very much."

His hand came back to her hair, and even though they were more than a foot apart on the couch, he played with the strands, keeping them connected in a way that felt good. "I'm sorry you lost him."

The words were sincere and the lump that formed in her throat was one of an old wound that would never go away. "Thank you."

"How did he die?" His voice was soft, and she got the sense he'd never push her to talk about it if she didn't want to. At the same time, the fact he didn't pussyfoot around it and pretend her husband hadn't died was refreshing.

"He was killed overseas in Iraq. I was six months pregnant with the girls. He almost cancelled the trip, but I told him I'd be fine. Twins can come as early as that, so he was worried I'd go into labor. As it was, I didn't deliver the girls until I was in my eighth month."

She paused a minute before going on. "He was there covering the war. They never identified the people who stopped the truck he was riding in. He and his photographer and their escorts were all killed."

He didn't offer platitudes. "Are the girls still close to his family? Do they see them often?"

Lyra nodded. "His parents were against our marriage in the beginning. Not in the same way my parents were, but his parents came around the minute the girls were born.

And over time, the wounds healed and we've grown close. I wanted them to be able to know him through his family. His sister lives a few hours from here so they see her often. His parents are in Nashville, but we see them once a year or more."

"And your parents?" His hand trailed to her shoulder, his fingers moving in small circles as they talked. He dropped it down to where her hand sat on the couch and held her fingers loosely.

"That rift hasn't been as easy to heal."

"No?"

She offered him a sad smile. "There were things said when Caleb and I got married that can't be taken back and can't really be forgotten."

"You don't have to talk about it if you don't want to. I didn't mean to bring up something . . . " He let the offer trail off but Lyra shook her head. She'd talked to her friends about this plenty. It hurt knowing her parents' feelings, but she had dealt with it in her own heart a long time ago.

"When Caleb and I got together, his parents had concerns, but mostly because they knew being in a biracial relationship can be hard. There are people in both our communities who weren't able to accept us. Their concerns came from a place of love." She hesitated, thinking about how to explain, and she glanced at the hallway leading to the bedrooms. She never wanted the girls to hear this. "For my parents and grandparents, it was different. My grandfather told me that I was a princess to Caleb. That marrying me would be a gift to him, but I'd have to bear the price of that for the rest of my life. That my kids would be marked with negro features, a wide nose and frizzy hair. My parents didn't say as much, but I could see they agreed. And they didn't defend me or Caleb. Didn't denounce the blatant

racism. I'm honestly not sure which was worse. My grandfather who spoke the words or my parents who did nothing to
negate them."

Now Luke's gaze shot to the hallway, too, and she felt a
pang at the protective gleam she could see in his eyes.
"Those girls? Those girls are gorgeous."

Lyra smiled. "Yes, they are. I worry, though. I guess
every parent does, but sometimes . . . " she shook her head
and the smile dropped. "I was so naive before I met Caleb. I
mean, I knew black Americans faced racism, but I really
had no idea how institutionalized and prevalent it was. As a
mother, it becomes all too apparent. It's things you never
realize are an issue until you're faced with it. Did you know,
black people are half as likely to be given pain medication as
a white person in an emergency room?"

The look on Luke's face said he was as shocked as she
had been when she saw the study. "Why?"

Lyra went palms up. "No one really knows for sure.
Some evidence points to a perception that black people are
more able to tolerate pain, although there's absolutely no
evidence of that. Others point to a perception of black
people as addicts. When someone is perceived as an addict,
it's harder to accept a claim they're in pain and need opioid
medicine to address it. Another study pointed to a general
belief that black people have thicker skin than white
people." She shrugged trying to cover just how angry it
made her. "Thicker skin, less pain."

"Wow."

"I know. Crazy, isn't it? I mean, I know they're going to
face challenges, but when you begin to examine it, it's really
shocking. For example, in one study in New York City,
black girls made up twenty-eight percent of the whole
student body, but they made up ninety percent of those

expelled from school. Whether the actors behind those numbers realize they're acting on racial bias or not, you can't deny the numbers. And, it's subtle things too. In many stores we shop at, there's a 'beauty' aisle and then there's the 'ethnic' aisle." She realized she'd gotten on a bit of a soap box. "I'm lecturing you, aren't I?"

Luke's expression was fierce when he shook his head. "You're their mama bear."

"I am. But I can't follow them out into the world. I can't go with them on job interviews or be there when they interact with the outside world. Frankly, my whiteness protects them if we make a trip to the emergency room. I can stand up and make sure they get the pain medicine they need. I can be an advocate for them at school. But someday, I have to let them go."

Luke chuckled. "Let me tell you, that's not easy. I worry for Naomi every minute of every day. It's hard having her so far from home."

"How's she doing?" She knew he talked to Naomi every few days, at least.

"Good. She likes her classes, for the most part, and she seems to have made a few good friends. She seems happy when I talk to her."

Lyra laughed. "And you still want to run up there and check on her, don't you?"

He grinned. "If she'd gone to school close by, I'd probably accidentally run into her on campus a few times a week. It would have been bad."

"You're a good man to admit that would have been a problem." She was laughing now, too.

"Hey," he looked chagrined. "I can admit I have a problem. I might not be able to fix it, but I can always admit to the problem."

She shook her head at him, but as the laughter faded, she realized he was watching her mouth now. Almost as intently as she'd studied his earlier, and a distinct heat sparked between them, weighty in the air.

"Right now, for example," he leaned closer to her and the air charged again, arousal and the fluttering resettling in her tummy before moving distinctly south, "I'm having a problem resisting your mouth. I'm not going to be able to fix the problem, but I'm well aware of it."

She had no response, but none was needed as he took her mouth with his. His mouth was soft, but it was firm, too, and there was no hesitation as he moved his lips over hers, easing her lips apart. She didn't try to fight it. She leaned in, her whole body wanting to be part of what was happening. He made her feel things she wasn't sure she'd ever felt with another man.

His tongue touched hers and the heat sparked to fire, banking further as his hand threaded through her hair and he pulled her close. She loved when he did that. It made her feel wanted. Desired and desirable because of it. When she wasn't in his arms, she had occasionally wondered what he'd think of her body. She'd delivered twins, after all, and she'd never completely gotten rid of the tummy bulge that had resulted from that.

But the minute his hands and mouth where on her, that hesitancy was forgotten. There was no analyzing, no worry, no feeling she might not be enough. With every touch, he told her again and again that she was enough.

She didn't know if he deepened the kiss or if she did, but she didn't care. It didn't matter. What mattered was what the kiss was doing to her. It melted her defenses. She'd been cautious about a guy who seemed too good to be true. About getting involved with someone at a time in her life when she simply wasn't ready to be involved with someone.

Those worries all flew out the window as the touch of his hands on her and his mouth teasing and tantalizing lit up every erogenous zone she seemed to have. He slowed the kiss, drawing it to a close, but so slowly, that the very tempo of it was teasing. As though he knew it would only make her want more. When he finally did end the kiss, he rested his forehead on hers, but kept his arms around her, maintaining the closeness.

"Wow." He breathed rather than spoke the word, the gruff undertone to his voice evidence of the effect the kiss had had on him.

"Uh huh." She heard the breathless quality in her own voice but wasn't surprised at it. The surprise came from the intensity of the kiss. She'd expected kissing him to be incredible, but this was so much more. "Wow."

CHAPTER TWELVE

Billy stared at the screen. "No." He tapped the keys, all the while trying to deny what he was seeing. "No, no, no, no, no."

Repeating the word wasn't doing dick.

He'd decided to lock down all the information, lock the whole freaking Brain Trust down, until he could talk some sense into Damon.

But that plan had failed the minute he tried to login. He couldn't. He'd been locked out. He was about to grab the phone and dial when an instant message popped up on his screen. Image file after image file came through and he stared at the screen. He couldn't be seeing this. This could not be happening.

"Fuck!" He shoved his chair back from the desk and held his head in his hands. "Fuck!"

On the screen, the message from Damon showed the true depths to which his one-time friend had been willing to sink. Not only had his partner managed to lock him out of the Brain Trust, securing the information and any information Billy might be able to find on the auction Damon was setting up behind his back, he'd planned all of this from the start.

The images on the screen showed that the whole thing had been set up to track back to Lyra. His partner had known just how to control Billy. Accounts, the ISP address, several of the fake accounts they'd been using, had been set up to look like Lyra had been the one to set them up and use them.

How was this possible? How the hell had Billy missed this? His leg bounced up and down as he weighed his next move. This couldn't be happening.

Bullshit he typed in the instant messaging box. Damon had to be bluffing. No way Billy missed this.

Try me was all the response he got.

The truth was, he couldn't try him. He couldn't call his bluff. And this asshole knew it. He couldn't mess around where Lyra was concerned. He needed to find a way to protect her. No matter what it cost him.

CHAPTER THIRTEEN

Joel looked as sick as Billy felt. "How did he do this?" He banged on some more keys on the computer in his office. The building was silent and dark, but for the lights they'd turned on in Joel's office.

"Can you undo it? Is there some way to delete everything? Erase . . . logs, or whatever?" Billy had dragged Joel out of bed and told him what he and Damon had done. The way they figured it, Damon had to have logged into Lyra's computer remotely from Joel's company computer.

Joel shook his head and waved his hands at the computer. "I don't . . . I can't . . . I don't know how to do that. I mean, I can see someone logged in and accessed her home computer on days she wasn't in the office. I can delete the logs, but the whole system is backed up to a remote backup."

"Can't you log into the backup?" Billy looked over Joel's shoulder.

"I can, but there's always some copy somewhere. The

cops will be able to find the trail, and if I erase it all, they'll see I erased it. I can't fucking do that, Billy."

Billy grabbed at the keyboard, sliding it his way. "We can't let Lyra go down for this either." He knew Joel was pissed, and more than a little hurt. Billy and Damon had done this without him, and it was big. Really big.

But they'd known Joel wouldn't be able to keep his mouth shut. Joel was constantly trying to impress Lyra. He'd tell her in a heartbeat what they were doing, and she would have come down on Billy for it. Even before Damon's fucked up plan to sell the information they'd collected to the highest bidder, Billy had known Lyra wouldn't approve of what they were doing. It wasn't like they were the ones violating non-disclosure agreements and shit, but it was sketchy. There had to be some sort of collusion charges or some shit that could be brought against them. Or maybe civil suits. They hadn't hacked into any systems or anything.

Of course, after the shit Damon had pulled with the trains, they could no longer argue they hadn't crossed the line into breaking the law. Billy ran a hand through his hair. Hell, for all he knew, they'd broken the law before that. He'd told himself they hadn't, but he just didn't know anymore.

Joel tore the keyboard back and they wrestled for a minute, but Joel shouted at him, butting through the panicked haze in Billy's head.

"Cut it the fuck out, Billy!"

Billy released his hold on the keyboard and sank back, leaning his whole body on the wall behind him. He felt exhausted all of a sudden, like he'd run a marathon. He let his head fall back and closed his eyes, listening to ragged breaths.

"I'm sorry, man, but we can't fix this shit from here. Not

without someone who knows what the hell they're doing. And, that's not me. You know I'd do anything to help Lyra, but I don't know how to fix this, dude."

They sat in silence, Billy wishing like hell he could go back and undo the last year. Joel was the one to break the silence.

"What about going to someone in the group? You said they're all geniuses. Aren't some of them capable of fixing this?"

Billy swallowed and raised hopeless eyes to Joel. "Yeah. They could, but what the hell would I tell them. Hey, we lied to you, pretended to be with you in the group, were out to fuck you over and make a buck on you. You probably would have lost your job once the company found out what you did? But fuck it, help me save my sister anyway. For old times' sake?"

Joel looked away with a small, "yeah."

"I fucked up so bad." Billy almost whispered the words. He didn't think he'd ever felt so dammed helpless in his life.

"Do you think Damon will really go through with it?" Joel's voice said he knew the answer but was hoping Billy could convince him he was wrong.

Billy met Joel's eyes. "Yeah, I do. I think he's changed lately. I don't think he much cares who he hurts anymore."

"I'm not sure he ever did," Joel said and Billy knew he was thinking back to times when Damon had bullied other people at campus parties or cheated to make a grade he knew he couldn't make. It wasn't something they'd ever talked about directly, but Billy could admit now, they'd made a lot of excuses for Damon over the years.

"I'll lose the company, won't I?" Joel looked around the office. "You know, I haven't had to take money from my dad to support this place in over a year."

"Shit. I'm sorry, Joel. But I'll tell the cops you had nothing to do with it." He knew he needed to go to the cops. He couldn't avoid it now.

"The publicity alone will kill us, even if they buy that I didn't know Damon was coming in here doing this."

"How do you think he did it?"

Joel shrugged. "He has the alarm code and it wouldn't have been hard for him to grab my keys and get a copy made some time."

They all had the alarm code to the building. Joel wasn't exactly careful with it. If his hands were full or he was a little drunk when they swung by the office to grab petty cash or whatever, he'd tell them to punch in the code. As far as Billy knew, he hadn't changed the code in three years.

Billy blew out a breath and walked back over to the computer. "All right. Let's look at the times he logged in. See if we can figure shit out. We'll print out the logs. Maybe at the very least, we can show you and Lyra weren't in the building at the time."

CHAPTER FOURTEEN

Lyra grinned as she watched Luke walk down the hall. The sight of his retreating back and . . . assets . . . was enough to make her grin, but the fact he had one of the girls hanging from each of his arms was the real source of the smile. The girls, for their part, were shrieking as he swung them back and forth. His biceps flexed under their weight but he didn't seem to strain in the least to hold them up.

Luke's laughter floated back to her and she moved to catch up to them, jogging the last few steps before inserting her key in the lock. They'd taken the girls out for pizza and stayed out later than she'd planned. Any hesitation she had at letting Prentiss and Alyssa grow attached to a man who might not be in her life on a long-term basis was starting to flit away. He was exceptionally good at getting her to let down her defenses. Besides, with him living across the hall, the girls saw him several times a day anyway. There was little point in trying to keep them apart.

Still, she would need to be sure her daughters understood Luke was only here for a short time. That way, if he ended up wanting to continue to see her after he moved out of the building, the girls could be pleasantly surprised. If not, they'd have been prepared for the absence ahead of time.

She was pretty sure she was telling herself that as much as she planned to tell the girls. She wanted to protect her heart against this man, in case he decided this was a temporary stop for him.

"Okay girls, you can stay up and watch a few minutes of television if you make it into jammies and brush your teeth in two minutes." She raised her phone and counted down. The girls knew the routine and thought the race was fun. "Three, two, one, and go!"

Twenty minutes later, the twins were in bed and she and Luke sat on the couch. The look he offered her now was one that said he was glad they were finally alone. She had to admit she was, too. As much as she loved them, being a single mom to young twins meant she didn't have a whole lot of time to herself, much less time being an adult. And she had a feeling what Luke had in mind was very, very, adult.

He reached one hand out and pulled her closer to him. Not that she needed much convincing, but the way he pulled her into him was enough to kickstart a small flame in her stomach. Who was she kidding? It was a lot lower than her stomach.

"You know I really like spending time with your girls, right?" His voice was deep and he leaned in, almost breathing the words as he nuzzled her neck.

"But this . . . " she said.

"But this . . . " he echoed and closed his mouth on the spot he'd discovered the night before. The spot that always seemed to make her weak-kneed and panting. He moved his mouth across her neck, masterfully, and she couldn't help the small mewl that came from her lips.

"God, I love the little sounds you make," he said, his mouth dropping to her shoulder.

"I love the way you make me make little sounds," she said, a small laugh coming from her. She didn't laugh long. Instead, she flexed toward him, and he answered by pulling her onto his lap. Large hands held her in place as he took the kiss to new levels and she prayed the girls wouldn't come out of their rooms for anything. She wasn't ready to sleep with Luke, but she could do this with him for, oh, an hour. Or twenty.

Luke's hands travelled up her torso, his thumbs slipping beneath the fabric to tease at the skin. She couldn't stop the press of her hips into him if she tried. She didn't.

Her whispered name was an oath on his lips as his hands worked over her breasts. Even through the layer of fabric her bra provided, the touch of his hands shot through her, awakening parts of her body that had lied dormant for a long time. Parts of her soul, too, if she were being honest.

"Luke," she pleaded, and she felt the curve of his smile on her lips as he answered.

"Yes, Lyra?"

"More, please." Her hips rocked into him again and this time, he ground up against her center, grasping her hips to hold her in place. His mouth didn't leave hers, hot and hungry, as he rode her through their clothing like horny teenagers in the back of a car. Part of her couldn't believe they were doing this. The other part was screaming at her to shut up.

She didn't listen to either part for long. Her brain turned to mush as the sensations in her body took over.

Luke freed the button on her pants and slid his hand, palm against her stomach, thumb slipping into her panties.

She let out a cry he managed to muffle with his mouth as his hand went south, but the pants were stopping him from getting to where she desperately needed him to be. He lifted her and moved so swiftly, it felt like she blinked and she was lying flat on her back on the couch, with Luke working her pants off her hips.

He moved pillows and stretched out beside her. "I won't take it any further," he whispered, a gruff ache in his voice. "I just need to see you come, Lyra."

He paused a beat, she guessed to see if she would protest. She wasn't stupid. She wasn't planning to protest a damned thing. She was too mindless for that right now. She snaked her arms around his neck and pulled him to her.

And then his mouth was on hers and his hand found the heat and wetness between her legs. His fingers didn't hesitate as he brought her to a mind numbing orgasm with startling speed. She clutched his shirt as her body shook in his arms and a moan crossed her lips.

When the waves of pleasure passed, he held her, nuzzling her neck as her breath evened out.

"God, you're beautiful, Lyra. So damned beautiful."

Warmth spread through her and she met his eyes. "I was worried."

He pulled back, meeting her gaze. "About what?"

She pressed her lips together but he waited, and she had a feeling he wasn't about to let her off the hook. The man probably also had the patience to wait her out. "I've had two babies. My body isn't quite, I mean it's just that . . . "

His eyes narrowed and intensity swamped his gaze. "You're beautiful. Trust me." He pressed his erection against her thigh. "See?"

She laughed at the playful grin that took over his face.

It took more time than it should have for the soft knocking to break through the haze in Lyra's head. She was completely wrapped up in the feel of Luke's arms around her, of his hands on her, his mouth on her neck, her lips. The feel of his hard length pressing into her as she straddled him. That kind of thing did things to a woman's ability to focus on interruptions, especially when they were definitely not welcome ones.

Luke pulled back and frowned at the door. "Is that your brother?"

Lyra sat up with a jolt. He was right. That was her brother calling to her through the door in the kind of stage whisper meant to see if she was awake and inside without waking the girls.

"Damn," she said, as she climbed off Luke's lap with his help, the absence of his hands on her markedly depressing. "What the hell, Billy?" She asked rhetorically.

Luke stood and gestured over his shoulder as Lyra pulled her pants back on. "I'll wait in the kitchen."

She nodded. They were on the same page. She'd ditch Billy. Fast.

Lyra waited until Luke had gone into the small kitchen before opening the door with a scowl. She loved her brother. He'd been there for her all these years when her parents hadn't been, but that didn't mean she wouldn't kick him out. She hadn't been with a man in … well, in far longer than she cared to acknowledge, even to herself.

One look at Billy stopped her short. He looked awful. His hair stuck out in all directions and he looked almost like he'd been crying. If she didn't know better, she might think he had. Her brother wasn't that type, though.

Her thoughts went to her parents. She might not be able

to forgive them for their attitude toward Caleb and her daughters, but on some level, she still loved them. If something had happened to them, the news would cut deep.

"What happened? What's wrong?" She asked the question as she moved aside to let him in.

"I'm so sorry, Lyra. I'm so sorry." As he spoke, she realized he held a stack of papers in his hand and she glimpsed the logo for Joel's company on the corner of the top page.

Lyra moved in front of him, stopping his movement. "Sorry for what? You're scaring me, Billy. What happened?" Something tight and heavy balled in the pit of her stomach and all thoughts of making out with Luke vanished. With some surprise, she realized she wanted to call Luke out here, to have him by her side for this, his strong presence helping as her brother seemed to crumple before her eyes.

Billy sat heavily on the couch and looked up at her. "I fucked up Lyra. I really fucked up. But I'm going to make it right."

Lyra sat next to him. Mothering two young twins alone had taught her a few things. One was that things were rarely as bad as people thought they were when they were in the thick of it. Sure, she'd never seen Billy as worked up as this, but she'd get him to explain what was going on and they'd work it out, together.

Unease spread through her chest as she looked at him and glanced back to the stack of papers. "Tell me, Billy."

He didn't look at her as he spoke. "I'm going to make it right, Lyra. I promise. Me and Damon have been working on a . . . " He seemed to struggle with how to explain things. "A business. The short story is that we've been collecting information from different companies."

The unease left her chest and flowed through her body,

prickling at her scalp. Collecting information. She knew that was Billy's way of saying they'd gotten something they weren't supposed to have through means they shouldn't have used to get it. Billy wanted a shortcut in life. He always had. If he had information, he'd gotten it the wrong way.

"What kind of information? What companies?"

Now he glanced at her, but quickly looked away. Her pity for him was gone. Because something told her this was about to tie back to her in some way. That he was going to need her to bail him out. Sure, he'd bailed her out plenty over the years by sitting for her when she needed help. By coming over and giving her breaks when the girls were sick. By being her extra set of hands. But bailing Billy out always meant something different. It meant truly bailing him out of trouble when he made stupid choices that left him in bad spots.

"Computer companies, defense contractors, bioengineering facilities, research labs." He ran his hand through his hair again and blew out a breath. "The kind of companies that have information that shouldn't get out there."

Her mouth dropped open and he raised his hands in defense. "We wanted to see what we could get and then go to the companies with it. Tell them how to plug their leaks."

"For a price," she said, realization dawning on her. "That's illegal, Billy."

"We're not hacking into the companies." This was said with indignation and she didn't want to know how he'd justified this in his head.

She purposely tried to relax her jaw. "Then how are you getting the information?"

"Their employees are giving it to us."

She raised a brow. She didn't need to ask him why

they'd simply turn over that kind of information. The question was written on her face.

"We're running fake scenarios in a private online group. We collect information as people release it in these hypotheticals. In the end, we're doing the companies a favor. These people are leaking information they've signed nondisclosures about. Some of them have military clearances. The faster these companies find out who can be trusted and who can't, the better."

Lyra closed her eyes for a minute, trying to resist the urge to shake him. He was older than her, but you wouldn't know it at times.

"Only . . ." He didn't continue and she wasn't sure she wanted him to.

She waited as he met her gaze with pleading eyes.

"Damon has gone off on his own. He's selling the information to some bad people. Really bad people." He looked sick and she felt a small amount of pity for him, but mostly she felt fear. Just fear and anger at him for being so damned stupid.

"You need to stop him."

"I can't. Oh God, Lyra, I can't. He's locked me out of things and he's set up everything . . . He's set it all up to look like you were behind things. He didn't make it obvious, but if the police go looking, it's going to come back to you as the ISP holder for the chat group online. He logged into your computer from Joel's office. Joel might be implicated."

The cold that ran through Lyra was unlike anything she'd felt since she was told Caleb had been killed.

Until she heard the deep voice coming from the kitchen. In that moment a whole new level of cold washed over her and she felt her world tip on its axis.

CHAPTER FIFTEEN

Luke stepped from the shadows of the kitchen. He could let Billy keep talking. Let him incriminate himself further, but there was no need. What he needed to do now was to get things taken care of to get Lyra's name cleared and to stop Damon from selling the information. He'd help Billy out as best he could—help him cut a deal for less jail time, but the information and Lyra took priority now.

"They already have, Billy." He said the words, knowing it would shove a wall between himself and Lyra that likely couldn't be torn down, but he couldn't do what he needed to do to save her and keep her name out of this unless he got Billy to talk. Got him to help take down Damon and any other accomplices out there. "They've got her name and the evidence tying her to the auction. I'll need you to come in with me and tell me everything you can so I can take down your accomplices and keep Lyra out of this."

He didn't look at Lyra. Couldn't. Because the look on her face was visible from the corner of his eye. She looked sick. Betrayed. Slain. And he'd done that.

Lyra didn't speak, but Billy did. "What the fuck? You're a cop."

Luke shook his head. "Not a cop. I'm not even on the books. But you'll be dealing with the military on this one." He glanced to Lyra now and held her gaze. "I'll help you all I can. We'll talk to the right people. But you'll need to tell them everything. Do everything they ask."

Billy was nodding and Luke looked back to him. "I can't make it go away, but I can try to help you if you help us stop the auction. Help us get your buddy and maybe lure a few of the buyers in too, if we can do that safely." Luke spoke evenly, even as his chest felt like someone had run a truck straight through it.

Lyra was looking at him, but there wasn't anger or rage or hurt in her eyes. Those gorgeous eyes that had been so lit with passion and heat moments before were now flat. Dead. She'd shut him out as surely as if she'd simply carved out the past few weeks and made him disappear from her life.

He'd thought it would feel good to be back to doing something with purpose, something that could make a difference in peoples' lives. And, shit, it should. If they could stop this auction, keep this information from getting out, he'd save thousands, if not millions, of lives. Not many could say that was all in a day's work.

Instead, he felt hollow.

CHAPTER SIXTEEN

Lyra watched in stunned silence as Luke led Billy from her apartment. There were no handcuffs, no officers to escort him out. Her brother simply walked out with Luke by his side.

It took her a minute to process what had just happened and kick into gear. She needed to get Billy a lawyer. She needed to get down to the police station and figure out how to protect her brother through this.

"Wait," she said to the empty room. Luke had said he wasn't even on the books. This was military, he'd said. What the hell did that mean? And where would he take her brother?

"Crap, crap, crap," she whispered, still quite aware of her sleeping girls in the next room. She was in no shape for them to wake up and see her. A bitter laugh bubbled out. How different the circumstances were from only half an hour before, where them waking up might have meant finding her and Luke messing around on the couch.

Lyra glanced at the clock and prayed her friend would still be up. She texted a quick nine-one-one "call me" message to Tracy and then turned her cell phone ringer down while she stared at her phone, waiting for the call.

Moments later, the call came and she swiped her thumb across the screen to connect it.

"Hey, what's up?" Tracy said, not sounding at all perturbed at the late hour.

"I need you to call Neil for me, please." Tracy's ex, Neil, was a lawyer. They'd had a hell of a battle during the divorce, so Tracy wouldn't call him lightly, but she also knew Lyra wouldn't ask lightly, either.

There was no hesitation in her friend's response. "Absolutely. What should I tell him you need?"

Lyra hated the shaking in her voice when she answered. "I don't know." She told Tracy everything that had happened in the last hour and listened to Tracy's short rant about Luke being a rat-fink bastard.

Lyra closed her eyes. She wasn't thinking about that part of the whole thing yet. She was choosing to focus on Billy, because focusing on Luke would hurt too damned much. Acknowledging the betrayal would make it too real, and she simply wasn't ready to face that yet. She had stupidly let herself feel something for the man, even though she didn't truly know him yet. That had been foolish, but she'd deal with that later.

"I'll call Mitch right now. I'm going to get Savvy to come there to be with you." Tracy and Savannah lived in neighboring apartments. Lyra knew Tracy would take the monitor from Savannah's and sit in the hallway to listen for either of their kids. She'd sit awake as long as Savvy needed to be with Lyra, even if it meant they all went to work exhausted the following day. They were family. It's what they did.

Lyra nodded even though Tracy couldn't see it. "Thank you." She whispered the words.

CHAPTER SEVENTEEN

Luke shut everything out as he and Billy walked to his car. When he'd gotten in, Luke placed a call to his brother.

"Yo." Zach didn't sound like he'd been sleeping at all.

"I need a safe house. You have something I can use?"

It wasn't unusual for officers or agents from other jurisdictions to use a safe house, or even a jail cell overnight, when they were passing through cities or towns. But Luke wasn't in a position to call the local PD and ask for help in this scenario. He needed someplace he could stick Billy and someone he trusted to watch him. That meant Zach. As much as he hated to put his brother in the position he was about to stick him in, it had to be done.

Zach was quiet for a minute before answering. "Not anything off the books. Come to my place."

"Is Shauna there?" It was bad enough he was putting Zach in this position. He wouldn't put his brother's girlfriend's job in jeopardy, too. Shauna was a detective for the state of Connecticut, clearing cold cases in a specialized unit.

"No. She had to run to New York to chase a lead. Won't be home until sometime tomorrow," Zach answered.

"Can you take off for a few days? I need extra eyes right now."

"You're working without backup?"

"Without backup, without a net, without a damned thing. And there are . . . complications." Most notably, his feelings for a gorgeous woman and her incredible girls. He couldn't let Lyra get hurt in all this. "See you in five."

Luke hung up and started the car, glancing at Billy. Sure, Luke could take him to the commander. But right now, Luke's priority was to clear Lyra. He would close down the auction, too, but he planned to protect Lyra and the girls first. The Commander would consider Lyra expendable and worry about whether she was innocent or guilty later. To hell with the consequences to her girls or her life in the meantime.

It's what Luke would have done at one time, too. Collateral damage couldn't always be helped when you were up against the kind of shit they fought against. But, apparently, sometime in the past eight years—or, hell, maybe in the past two months—his priorities had shifted.

Billy was looking a little bug-eyed and Luke knew the kid had to be freaking. He'd played a dangerous game, and he'd lost. To his credit, he was standing up and doing what needed to be done now. It wasn't much but it was something.

When they arrived at Zach's place, his brother opened the door as they approached and glanced outside when they entered. Luke pulled him aside and gave him a three-minute rundown of the case he'd been working under the radar. His brother's eyebrows met the sky, but he didn't comment. Luke had a feeling he'd be hearing some shit later, but that could—and would—wait.

Zach leaned against the doorjamb, taking in everything even as he looked for all the world like he was simply standing casually. One shoulder held the wall up, but Luke knew his brother was ready to move the instant it became necessary. It shouldn't. Billy was too motivated to protect Lyra at this point to try something stupid.

"Let's start with whose dumb ass idea this was and who's involved," Luke said, putting a recorder out on the table between he and Billy. He wasn't detaining Billy. The kid was free to go if he wanted to, so there wasn't any need right now to worry about rights or lawyers or shit like that.

"It was my idea, but this wasn't how it was supposed to be." Billy's eyes pleaded, but Luke just waited for him, neither absolving nor judging, for now. "It was supposed to be a way to get other people to hack shit for us. Me and Damon aren't hackers, but we were able to get all these people to tell us backdoors and secret weaknesses of their companies."

"Tell me who else was involved. Who set up Lyra?" Luke saw Zach's gaze flick to his, then back to Billy's.

"Damon. Damon Taylor."

Luke saw Zach take out his phone and begin to text. "Off the record, Zach," he shot to his brother who answered with a nod, not looking up. Luke looked back to Billy and nodded for him to continue.

"Damon and me went to school together. He's wicked smart, but no one realizes how smart he is. I guess I didn't either. I never thought he'd fuck with my sister like this."

"Was Joel involved?"

"No. He didn't know anything about it. We knew he wouldn't have the stomach for it. Or he'd blab about it to

Lyra and she would have flipped." Billy glanced away. Maybe he should start using whether Lyra would flip or not as his criteria for what to do in life, Luke reflected.

"When did Damon start setting up the auction?" Luke knew the answer to this but wanted to see how much Billy knew.

"I don't know, man." He raised his hands, palms out, to stress his innocence. "Honest to God, first I found out about it was the train thing. As soon as I saw that, I knew. I just knew. I recognized it from the groups."

Luke shifted in his seat and avoided looking at his brother. He would never get past the role he played in that. It had been necessary. That he knew. But it would stay with him.

"Soon as I saw that," Billy went on, "I called Damon. That's when he told me he wasn't taking the information to the companies like he'd planned."

"And Damon locked you out of things?" Luke asked.

Billy's nod was miserable. "Yeah. I can't get into anything. Joel tried, too, but he couldn't get in either. Joel owns a company that works with computers and programming and all that shit, but he doesn't know all that much as far as that shit goes. His dad just funded the company. I think his dad even told him what to do, said computers would treat him right, or some shit. Turns out, the business was actually making a go of it."

"So how did Damon succeed in setting up Lyra?" Luke picked up the papers Billy had printed out and looked through them again. They weren't good.

"He used the computers at Joel's office to remotely log in to Lyra's computer." He gave a nod to the papers. "I'm hoping we can prove she was someplace with witnesses when these things happened. Maybe I can clear her that way."

Luke nodded. "So, Damon has enough computer knowledge to do that? To set things up in Lyra's name and to get into Joel's computer?" Luke asked. Something wasn't adding up about that.

Billy shrugged. "He said he was handling it. He must have because I didn't do it. I swear I didn't set her up. We both had identities in the room so we could talk to the people and milk them for shit. Get them to talk. Damon was the one that killed it at that, though. He's good at fucking with people's minds. He made them feel like what they were doing was safe. He'd tell me what to do most of the time, like if I should act like I was giving up info or whatever with one of my fake identities so one of the people in the room would get more comfortable and start to open up. Once they saw someone else doing it, it became easier for them to spill their secrets. Or sometimes he'd tell me to taunt someone a little or something while he played the supportive card, or whatever. Damon knew all that. I guess I didn't want to see it, but the more I think about it, the more I realize if he's fucking with peoples' heads, he's happy."

Luke looked to Zach. "Any chance we can get someone to help us with the computer side of things?" He lowered his voice. "Maybe Sam can help?"

Zach nodded and stepped into the kitchen. If his brother could get ahold of Samantha Stone and enlist her help and the help of her husband, Luke would feel a hell of a lot better about this. Samantha worked for a local company, but she was also one of the top hackers in the nation, if not the world. She often did freelance jobs for federal agencies, and had clearances to match. Her husband, Logan, was a former SEAL. He and Luke hadn't known each other on the teams, but they'd met several times since retirement, and Luke would trust Logan with his life. As backup went, the two would be hard to beat.

"How do you think Damon got into Joel's computer?" Luke looked back at Billy, knowing there was something they were missing here.

Billy shrugged. "That part was easy. Joel was never very careful with anything. Damon and I both have the alarm code to the building his offices are in and his computer passwords. We have for years. It would have been easy for Damon to use Joel's computer to access Lyra's home network." He lowered his head. "I never thought he'd try to put this on Lyra. Never."

"And you're sure Joel didn't help him?"

"No. He was shocked. He's pretty afraid his business is going to be implicated and he'll take the fall for some of this, but he had no idea. When I showed up there earlier, he was clueless."

Luke chewed on that. Was it possible Damon had pulled Joel in without telling Billy? Would Joel have wanted something to hold over Lyra's head? Maybe he thought he could come in and save her at the last minute, and win her heart that way? Maybe he didn't bet on Damon using the information before he did and things got out of control? Or maybe he planned to use the information to exert pressure of his own on her. The thought stoked the fire raging through Luke. He'd tear the asshole apart.

Billy's phone chimed an alert on the coffee table and Luke leaned in to pick it up before Billy could. What he saw when he swiped his finger across the screen took him a minute to process. It seemed like his head was fighting it, wanting it to be wrong so badly, it threw up roadblocks against the information. But there was no fighting it. His gut clenched and his heart seemed to stutter before locking up in his chest.

A picture had been sent to Billy. A picture of Lyra and the girls. And what Luke saw in the picture sent him over the edge. He was on Billy in a heartbeat, a growl building from deep inside him as he erupted.

CHAPTER EIGHTEEN

Lyra smiled for the girls and told them she'd get them out of there and get them back home. Things had gone past the point where she could tell them it was all a game. The marks on her face were enough to scare the hell out of them and she knew this was something they wouldn't get over lightly, even if she got them out of it. Their own faces were tear-streaked and part of her wanted to launch herself at Damon and claw his eyes out for doing this to her girls.

Not if. When. When she got them out of this. She would get them out of this. Her thoughts flew to Luke and she prayed like hell he would be looking for them, but she wasn't one to sit and wait for a knight in shining armor to save her. Life had taught her that knights were often too busy riding their horses to do the real heavy lifting.

She had given herself ten minutes to curse herself for opening the door without checking to see who it was at such a late hour. Truthfully, she couldn't really beat herself up over that. When she'd seen it was Mrs. Lawson's nephew, Murphy, at her door, she'd been surprised to see him, but she hadn't thought anything was wrong. She'd been expecting to see either Neil or Savvy on her doorstep. She'd talked to Neil by phone and he was trying to find out where Luke would have taken Billy and if he could get in to see him. The *if* part of that had thrown her. Surely, they'd let his lawyer in to see him? To represent him?

Apparently, when you engaged in acts that were arguably terrorism, things played out a little differently. Not to mention, she had no idea what agency Luke was even linked with. It struck her she wasn't even sure if that was his real name and she hated the fact that despite that, she was still hoping he would rescue them.

It had taken Lyra several seconds to react to the weapon in Murphy's hand, to process the fact he was holding a gun on her. He had pushed her into her apartment and shut the door before she could move. She'd tried to fight him when he'd made a move toward the hallway where Alyssa and Prentiss slept. They'd wrestled and she had clawed at his face, scratching him hard and drawing blood. It was only then that he'd struck her with the butt of the gun across the side of her head.

He'd looked almost sick at what he'd done. He even apologized. It hadn't kept him from rounding up her and the girls and threatening to shoot them if she didn't follow orders. If she didn't do exactly as he said and leave the apartment complex quietly with him.

Lyra shook off the memory and pulled the girls into her lap as she looked around them. The room was small and there was nothing more than the bed they sat on in it. She hesitated to describe it as a bedroom with its lack of windows and furnishings. She'd tried the door already. It was locked from the outside. There was nothing besides the bed frame in the room.

"They're fighting, Mama." Prentiss's voice was small and shaky and Lyra knew the muffled voices outside the door were scaring her. They were scaring Lyra, and she was an adult.

Lyra pressed her mouth close to Prentiss's ear. "It's all right, baby. Try not to listen to them." She glanced at the door and back down at the bed they were sitting on. The frame was a plain metal frame, the kind you could add to a mattress purchase for forty-nine-ninety-nine. If any of the bolts were loose, she might be able to get a leg or one of the bars that braced the mattress on the underside of the bed off. A hard enough crack in the head with it might take a man down.

Her thoughts were interrupted by the sounds of arguing. She knew the voices. One was Murphy and the other was Damon. She never would have dreamed Damon would hurt her or the girls, but she was absolutely sure it was him. Worse, he seemed to be in charge. At least, that's the way it sounded, given he was now telling Murphy to shut up and do what he was told. His voice was cold and hard, sending a shiver of dread through her.

She gestured with one finger over her mouth to the girls and then moved them down onto the floor. As quietly as possible, she slid beneath the bed and looked at the bottom side of the frame. Just as she'd hoped. On the frame she'd had like this in college, there had been an extra bar down the center that was connected on one side. It was made to swing into place if the user extended the bed to accommodate a queen-sized mattress.

Lyra worked her fingers over the bolt holding the one side to the frame, loosening it until it came off all the way. She slid the metal down onto the floor. Sliding out to sit next to the girls again, she wiped the small bit of oil that covered her fingers on the inside of her shirt before pulling the metal piece over close to her. It was still under the bed where the men wouldn't see it if they entered but she could grasp it if she needed it.

She played through scenarios in her head. The metal was long, about six feet. It wasn't too heavy. She'd be able to swing it, but it would do some damage if she could get the metal to connect with someone's head. Her best bet would be if some of the men left. If she was left with only one person to guard them at any point, she might be able to lure whoever it was into the room and strike.

Her eyes went to her girls again and she cringed at the idea of luring one of the men into the room where her girls were. It was one thing to take risks if it was just herself at stake. But what choice did she have? She could either sit here and hope someone rescued them, or maybe that the men let them go after they got whatever it was they wanted from Billy—or she could be ready to take advantage of any opportunity they had to get out of here alive.

She choked on the sob that threatened to make its way up her throat at the thought. No way would she let the girls see her cry. No way in hell.

CHAPTER NINETEEN

"Where, Billy? Where?" Luke ground the words out through clenched teeth.

Zach grabbed Luke from behind and hauled him off Billy. "If you kill him, he can't tell us anything."

Billy sat staring wide-eyed at Luke as he gasped for air. Luke didn't give a shit if the kid could breathe at the moment. He wasn't doing a very good job of breathing at the moment himself. He felt like someone had taken a sledgehammer to his chest.

Luke turned the phone to Billy again, showing him the picture of Lyra and the girls. The girls were crying. Lyra was bleeding.

Bleeding from a cut on her cheekbone around which an angry bruise was already forming. Luke recognized the injury. It would have come from someone striking Lyra. Striking her hard, maybe with the back of a hand, or a fist. Hard enough to cut open the flesh and have the side of her face swelling.

Billy looked sick at the sight and began to shake his head. "I don't know. I don't know."

Luke tipped back his head and swore. He had to figure out where they would take her.

"The text says he'd let them go," Billy said. "If I let them run the auction, they'll let them go and everything will be okay."

Luke shook his head at the kid. He might be an adult in years, but Luke had never looked at Billy and thought of him as anything other than a kid. His naïveté now was proving the point. No way Damon was going to just let her go once this was over. That shit simply didn't happen in real life.

"I'm going to see what Sam can do." Zach left the room. Luke knew his brother would need to call this in soon. He was a detective. He couldn't have evidence of an abduction and not let his superiors know about it. Not call in backup at all. With any luck, Luke could convince Zach to give him a head start before calling this shit storm in.

CHAPTER TWENTY

Damon waited. He could be patient. She was saying goodbye to friends and had been for the last half hour. It seemed like every time she said goodbye to one friend, another stepped up. He'd have to move quickly and be discreet.

The minute he met Lyra's new boyfriend, he'd known the guy had to be undercover. How she hadn't seen it, he'd never know. Then again, maybe she wasn't the suspicious type. Damon liked to think of it as cautious, self-preservation if nothing else.

When Billy said the guy had taken over the super's duties for a short time, Damon had started digging into the guy's life. It never hurt to be prepared and know just how to hit someone if you needed to go on the offensive. Luke Reynolds had an Achilles heel all right. A big one.

Damon kept his head down in a book and when someone tried to talk to him, he was polite, but brisk.

Finally, she was on the move again. Damon closed the book and tucked it under his arm, whistling as he walked toward her. She headed out toward the small parking lot and he jogged behind her.

"Naomi," he called out, raising a hand.

She turned and smiled, and he slid the gun between her arm and rib cage, making sure she could feel it press into her side.

He smiled. "Keep walking, keep smiling. You and I are going to take a little trip."

He could see her open her mouth and take a deep breath, but he tugged her closer, twisting his hand and digging in with the gun. "Scream and the twins are going to pay the price for it."

"The twins?" Her face gave her away. She knew exactly who he was talking about.

"Try me. I promise you. You'll regret it," he bit out, still smiling and looking down at her, letting her see in his eyes that he didn't make idle threats.

He steered them to his car and it was done.

Patience always paid off.

CHAPTER TWENTY-ONE

The room outside grew quiet. Lyra needed to stand and stretch her legs again to keep the blood circulating. Getting stiff or having her legs fall asleep wouldn't be a good plan right now. The girls had fallen asleep though, each with a heavy head on her lap. She hated to wake them. Hated to have them go through the realization that this nightmare was anything but that. That it was really happening and they were still stuck in the dank room.

She heard movement in the room outside, maybe a chair scraping. Definitely the sound of footsteps. The footsteps weren't coming toward the room she and the girls were in, but she sat still, straining to hear them anyway. Lyra shook the girls awake, finger pressed to her lips as they sat up and stared at her. She wanted to cry when she saw their faces, saw dawning come. Saw the fear there as they remembered what had happened and where they were.

She didn't. She pressed them behind her and then stood, shaking her legs out as silently as she could, then sat again, her right hand sitting on the floor near where she'd stashed the metal bar under the bed. She needed to be ready to slide it out and use it if she needed to.

She didn't look at the way the girls huddled behind her. Doing that would break her heart.

The footsteps stopped for a bit and then began again, this time leading to the door to their room. She heard the lock turn and the door swung open. There was more light outside the room than in, leaving her looking at a silhouette, but she recognized it.

Murphy.

The girls crept into her lap but Lyra stared at Murphy, her right hand still ready to move if he came forward. She would need to stand in one motion, pulling the metal bar out without putting the girls down gently, but they shouldn't be hurt from the fall, if she needed to act. All of her being wanted to wrap her arms around them protectively, but she didn't dare.

He stood in the doorway for what seemed like an eternity, and Lyra could hear soft whimpers from Prentiss and Alyssa. In what seemed like an agonizingly slow move, Murphy slid a tray he'd been holding in one hand toward them, then scanned the room before shutting the door.

The girls were on the food in a heartbeat, before Lyra could think to stop them. They'd been given water bottles earlier in the day, but with those she'd been able to see that the seals on the bottles hadn't been cracked.

The girls were wolfing down peanut butter and jelly sandwiches before she could stop them, and Lyra closed her eyes and said a prayer that there wouldn't be anything in them to hurt the girls. She would let them eat their fill before eating any. They'd been hours without food.

"Slow down, girls," she said quietly. "You'll get a belly ache if you eat too fast."

Prentiss nodded and pushed a sandwich toward her mom.

Lyra shook her head. "You eat first, baby. I'll eat whatever's left over."

"I have to go potty, mom," Alyssa said, putting down the last of her third sandwich.

Lyra bit her lip and looked to the door and back. By the way Prentiss was crossing her legs and bouncing, she knew both girls had to go. So did she, for that matter.

Lyra crossed to the door and banged on it with her fist. "The girls have to go to the bathroom." She didn't use Murphy's name. She didn't want to remind him that she knew who he was and could identify him if he let them go free. It was something that had been hanging over her this whole time. She knew perfectly well that they were aware she could identify Damon and Murphy if they released her. She needed to find a way to convince them that she wouldn't do that.

Maybe if she talked to him about his grandmother. Got him to see how disappointed she'd be in him. What Lyra couldn't figure out was why in the world he'd be working with Damon. Murphy was a man who brought his grandmother her groceries once a week, for heaven's sake. What on earth would make him do something like this?

She heard footsteps coming toward them and stepped back from the door. It opened and Murphy glared at her, annoyed, then looked toward the girls.

"One at a time."

"No." Lyra spoke firmly. "We go together."

He stared her down and she wondered what the outcome of this would be if Damon were here. It had been clear to her that Damon was the one in charge.

"Fine." He stood back and let her and the girls come

through the door and out into the outer room. "Be fast about it, though. And no fucking around. I'll make you sorry if you fuck with me at all."

The words seemed out of place coming from him, as though he were a little boy playing in an adult's clothing. Like the fight with Damon had made him feel the need to prove himself to her.

Lyra moved out into the room, one twin on either side, pressed against her tightly. She realized with a start, the walls of the room they were in were all lined with some sort of heavy foam. Her eyes moved to a long desk with machinery on it and she recognized sound mixing equipment. They must be in a recording studio.

As Murphy swore and shoved her toward a dirty bathroom on the other side of the room, she realized something. A recording studio meant sound proof walls. Tears burned her eyes but she refused to let them fall. As she and the girls used the facilities, she took deep breaths. When she moved back through the room with them, she wanted to be ready to take in every detail she could. Everything from furniture placement to phones, weapons, exits. Every small scrap of information that might help her formulate a plan. She needed to stay calm to do this right.

Inside the bathroom, Lyra scooted the girls to the potty, while she quietly opened the drawers and cabinets, searching for anything that could be used as a weapon. There was very little there. The bottom drawer was filled with empty toilet papers rolls and a few crumpled tissues, as though it was being used as a garbage can. The next drawer up was empty.

The top drawer held dental floss and a substance that looked yellow, sticky, and gross. Lyra wasn't about to try to figure out what it was. As Prentiss and Alyssa switched places so Alyssa could go to the bathroom, Lyra opened the medicine cabinet. A bottle of Tylenol and black eye liner. It was the kind with a brush tip that was more like a marker than the typical crayon type of liner.

Alyssa finished using the bathroom and Lyra looked at the pen in her hand. She didn't want to think about what could happen to her, but if she and the girls were separated, she wanted a way for someone to get them help. A way to get them to safety if she was—

She swallowed and refused to think about what it would mean for her if someone had to use this. She turned Alyssa so her back was to her and lifted her shirt, writing Uncle Luke and Luke's cell phone number on her daughter's back. She waved the shirt back and forth to dry the liner as Murphy banged on the door for her to finish up.

Lyra reached over and turned on the faucet. "Almost done."

She repeated the procedure with Prentiss, not looking her girls in the eye as she did it, but she knew each of them watched as the words went on the other's back. She couldn't explain to them that they might be on their own if something happened to her. She couldn't do it.

CHAPTER TWENTY-TWO

"Sam's on it. She'd running property searches for Damon and for Joel, in case Damon is using one of his properties." Zach spoke to Luke as he walked back into the living room, not bothering to so much as acknowledge Billy's presence any longer.

Luke looked at his brother and scrubbed a hand down his face. "Listen, Zach, I know you need to call this in. Can you give me—" He broke off when his phone rang and he saw it was Naomi face-timing him.

Part of him wanted to let it go. She would see right off that something wasn't right with him. A tingle went up the back of his spine and he slid to answer her call, freezing when he saw the video. The room was dark, but the image of Naomi was clear. So was the gun that was held to her head.

Her voice was shaky when she spoke. "Uncle Luke—" She wasn't given a chance to finish. Damon appeared on the screen.

"A little birdy told me you're thinking of poking your

nose in where it doesn't belong." Damon held the phone so Luke could see the gun he pointed back at Naomi now as she sat, white faced and still beside him.

Damon continued talking as Luke soaked in every detail he could, but there wasn't much to be told. It looked like they were in a bathroom. It was filthy. Maybe a gas station or restaurant restroom. He could see dirty tiled walls and the kind of metal divider that made up the bathroom stalls.

"I don't like people butting into my business. Luckily, I'm always thinking one step ahead, and I had a little insurance plan in mind for just such an occasion. If you want to get your niece back in one piece, you'll sit back and let me do things my way."

Luke hated the look on Naomi's face, but he quickly realized she was mouthing something at him. He spoke to Damon, but kept his eyes on Naomi. "If you hurt one hair on her head, I'll tear your heart out and feed it to your fucking mother for breakfast."

It was cliché, but it was what he could come up with since his attention was divided. It didn't matter. As Damon grinned and told him his mother was dead and he'd be out of the country before Luke could get to him, Luke made out Naomi's words. She was repeating, "save the twins," over and over to him. *Save the twins.*

Damon must have run his mouth enough for Naomi to know he had Lyra and the twins, and she was telling him to go after the girls. That was how she was. It was the kind of person she was soul deep, and he loved that about her.

Damon disconnected and Luke looked up at Zach. He intended to save all of them. Naomi, the twins, and Lyra. And then he was going to take down this Damon asshole and all the people working with him.

CHAPTER TWENTY-THREE

"I'm not on the clock." Zach had been telling Luke the same thing for the last five minutes as they waited for Samantha and Logan to arrive. "I don't need to call in shit."

Luke raised his brows. He knew that was bullshit. Zach was putting his job at risk. Luke couldn't blame him. He'd do the same thing in Zach's shoes.

Zach stepped in front of him and stopped his pacing, speaking quietly. "Listen, Luke, I know this is killing you. You saw yourself as our family's caretaker long before the accident. And you stepped up in a way I couldn't have then. I wouldn't have had it in me to raise Naomi like you did. But I've got your back on this now. Sometimes taking care of the family means letting the family step up."

Luke nodded. "All right."

Luke scrubbed at his face. Something had been needling him. "He's got to be working with a partner."

"Why's that?" Zach asked.

"In the video, it was clear Damon was holding the

phone and it looked like it was only he and Naomi in the bathroom."

His brother looked at him for a beat. "So you're thinking he wouldn't have left Lyra and the twins somewhere without a partner to watch them?"

"It's too risky. He's organized, calculated. He knew about Naomi ahead of time. He planned what to do ahead of time to control Billy and I."

Zach shook his head. "Could have them tied up in a van somewhere. In a hotel room, an apartment."

"Maybe, but I don't think so. It's too risky. You leave her alone like that and she can try to signal to someone. Leave them in a van parked somewhere on campus while he grabs Naomi, all Lyra has to do is kick the sides of the van. Apartment or hotel room, same thing. She makes noise."

"Or he has them drugged. Or knocked out." Zach looked almost apologetic as he spoke. He didn't say the "or worse" they both knew belonged on the end of that sentence.

Luke turned to Billy. "Besides you and Joel, who else could Damon be working with. Who else could be involved in this?"

"I don't know, man. No one else was supposed to be in on it. It was just supposed to be us."

"What about Aiden James? You think Damon would have grabbed him? Pulled him in if he needed someone to help him get to Lyra?"

"The asshole that lives next to her? Hell no. Damon said that guy was a pervert."

The doorbell rang and Zach opened it to Logan and Samantha. The latter didn't look up from a small laptop she carried with one hand and typed on with the other as she made her way to the couch.

"Damon Taylor doesn't own any property and he seems to be estranged from his father. Mother is dead." Samantha spoke without preamble. Luke had always liked her. "Joel Sadoski has a couple of things we should check into."

Samantha glanced around now as she looked up and Luke nodded for her to continue. Logan stood at her back and Luke knew he'd go wherever they needed him to and do whatever needed to be done to end this. "Joel's dad has bought him a few businesses in addition to the one Lyra works for. That one leases office space at a building downtown. They'd be unlikely to take them there because the building is shared by a few other businesses. We can check it, but . . ."

"Skip it," Zach said.

"Before that business, he wanted to start up a music production company. It never really panned out, but he does own a small recording studio as a result. It looks like they let people rent the space, but it's not doing all that well. That would be my best guess for where they've got Lyra and the girls." Samantha looked up at the men as she spoke, then down to her computer again. "I'm still searching for anything out near Naomi's school."

They had relayed the news of Naomi's abduction to Samantha and Logan as soon as they had it. It killed Luke to know she was in trouble hours away where he couldn't get to her right away. He'd never felt so damned pulled in different directions in his life. Even when his sister had died and he'd had to face the reality of leaving the teams long before he was ready to, the decision had been a no-brainer. You took care of family. Always.

Right now, he felt like he had two families, and both of them were in danger.

Logan was the next to speak. "Chad and Jax are on the

way over. Zach, me and you should go get Naomi when we track down where they might have her. Luke, you can take Chad and Jax with you to get the girls and Lyra. They're both ex-military. Jax is a medic."

He didn't add that Jax's skill could be handy if any of them were hurt, but he didn't need to.

Luke nodded. It killed him to know he wouldn't be going after Naomi, but he also knew she cared what happened to the twins. She wouldn't forgive him if something happened to Lyra or the twins while he was saving her. Not any more than he'd forgive himself. The only problem was, the same could be said for the other way around. How the hell would he live with himself if Naomi was hurt, or worse, while he went after Lyra and the twins?

He took a slow deep breath, employing every damned skill in the field he'd ever had to calm himself down. One step. Then another. That was how they'd get through this. Just like when he'd been active duty.

The only damned problem was, he wasn't active duty and hadn't been in a long freaking time. What the hell had he been thinking? He was a washed up old SEAL who'd turned himself into a stay-at-home Mr. Mom. And now he'd be expected to save just about everyone he loved before his whole world was wiped out by some asshole who apparently didn't give a shit who he hurt so long as he could make a buck.

What could possibly go wrong?

CHAPTER TWENTY-FOUR

"Do we wait for Zach and Logan to locate Naomi before we move on the studio?" Jax Cutter looked to Chad and Luke. Zach and Logan had left to head toward Dartmouth while Samantha sat cross legged on the couch tracking down where Naomi might be.

Luke grimaced. The unspoken part of Jax's question was what would Damon do to Naomi if he either got word they'd freed Lyra and the twins, or even if he simply didn't hear from whoever he'd left here holding the girls.

Then again, Damon might have taken Lyra and the twins with him up to Dartmouth. He'd also said something about leaving the country. If he fled with any of the women or the girls . . . hell, Luke didn't want to think about it.

He needed to think strategically. "Let's get to the recording studio and see if we can spot anyone. If we get eyes on them and they're safe, we can hold off until Logan and Zach are in position." In position? They didn't even have any idea where Naomi might be held.

Chad nodded and turned to Sam. Chad was Samantha's boss at Sutton Capital, so the two were used to working together. "Keep looking and let us know as soon as you find something."

Samantha nodded but didn't look up. "If we could get ahold of Damon's credit card information—a statement maybe from his apartment—I can try to get into his accounts." Now she glanced up. "Just saying." She was pulling double duty, looking for any properties or clues to where Damon might have taken Naomi while trying to break into the cache of data Damon was holding for the auction. If she could, she'd secure the data somehow and see if she could shut down the auction remotely.

A knock on the door told them Jack Sutton had arrived. He'd be sitting with Samantha and Billy to be sure Billy didn't pull any shit and try to take off. Luke doubted he would try anything. He looked miserable sitting on the couch across from Samantha, answering occasional questions from her as she worked.

Who knew what he might try if it was just him and Samantha left, though. The guy was motivated by greed and a drive for easy money. It would be easy to see him trying to take off if he thought he could get out from under this by running.

Chad spoke in low tones to Jack after he'd shaken everyone's hands and been introduced to Luke.

When he'd been an operator on the teams, Luke had relied on the cold, steady calm that came over him as they went into an op. If you were ready, if your team was ready, if your plan had been vetted, you could achieve that calm. And it was a calm that served you well when you went into a battle and shit went sideways in a heartbeat. It was what let you think on your feet, move swiftly and decisively to a backup plan, or the backup to the backup plan. It was what kept you alive.

As he and Chad walked to the car, all he could picture was Lyra's beautiful face. He saw her looking up at him, those soft lips parted for him, eyes soft and accepting of everything about him. He saw the twins running down the hallway to him, ready to climb onto his shoulders or swing around on his arms. He could feel their trusting hands clinging to him, and he wanted for all the world to be the superhero they thought he was.

He could see Naomi as she'd waved to him when he'd dropped her at Dartmouth. He'd worried about her there, being far away from him and Zach. Never in a million years had he imagined something he would get involved in would follow her there and put her life in danger. The girl had been through more than enough in her young life. This was the very last thing she deserved.

As Chad drove, Luke clamped down on the swirling emotions that weren't serving him and swiped clean the images in his mind. He needed to shut off all emotion, to see the op from a strategic standpoint only. Get in, get the girls and Lyra, get out.

Two deep breaths and he was ready. Hands steady, heart and mind focused only on the job. When this was over, he could fall apart. For now, he was a SEAL again.

All in.

CHAPTER TWENTY-FIVE

They parked a block down from the recording studio and approached from three different directions. Luke didn't want to know why Chad had comms for all of them, but he did.

"I'm not seeing any movement." Chad's voice came over the earpiece. "You guys?"

"Not a damned thing," Luke said.

"Nothing here," Jax confirmed.

Luke moved forward. "Watch the front. I'm moving closer." He moved in on the building, keeping an eye out all around him, but the area seemed completely deserted. Of course, there could be a basement or interior room they were holding Lyra and the girls in.

There were no cars in the small lot at the back of the squat building. No signs of light or life coming from inside. He had a bad feeling they were in the wrong place. He moved smoothly to the back door. The windows were all dark and covered. There was no way he was getting a peek at what was inside from out here.

"Any windows?" Luke spoke quietly, but knew the men would understand what he was asking. Negative responses came from both of them.

Luke wanted eyes on Lyra and the girls and he wanted them now. He checked the knob of the back door. Locked.

"I'm gonna take a peek inside." He didn't wait for an answer from the others. He set about picking the lock on the back door and was inside a dark back hallway before either man objected.

He immediately wished Chad had night vision goggles in his little bag of tricks, but the man didn't strike Luke as a geardo—the term they'd used in the teams for guys who spent personal money on gadgets and gear they didn't have any tactical need for. Chad likely had the occasional need for comms in his work, but Luke doubted that need extended so far as to need night vision.

He flicked on the small flashlight he had in his pocket, then began to move silently down the hallway, using the angles to see into and clear rooms, weapon at the ready. He heard Chad announce his arrival in the front hall through his comms and grunted an acknowledgement.

Luke cleared a small bathroom and a closet, then bounced his flashlight over Chad's quiet form as the latter entered the hallway from the opposite end. They worked together toward the only other doorway in the space. It opened to an empty control room that held only two chairs and an old panel of controls and dials, presumably for adjusting volumes and sounds and whatever else they did when recording music. They could see the recording studio itself through a viewing window. It sat empty.

Luke eyed the foam on the walls of the recording studio and the control room and a new rage coursed through him. Sound proofing. Fury licked through his body. The assholes that had Lyra and the girls better not have had any damned need for that soundproofing. He'd shred the hell out of them if he found they had.

One door remained off the back of the room. With a nod, Chad and Luke approached and Chad put his hand on the knob. Luke nodded again, weapon raised as Chad swung the door wide. Luke's flashlight quickly bounced off the walls, checking all corners of the room. Nothing. An empty bed. Not the fierce brunette and smiling girls he'd hoped to find.

"They were here." Chad nodded to the scraps of sandwiches and bottled water that littered the floor.

"The question is," Luke growled, "where the hell are they now?"

CHAPTER TWENTY-SIX

Lyra held the girls tight as the van rocked into a turn. They'd been moving along a rutted road for the past few minutes. She knew that meant they were headed someplace remote, and the feeling didn't offer her any comfort at all. Murphy had suddenly entered the room and shoved them out the door and into a van without telling her what they were doing or why they were being moved.

The girls seemed to be shut down. They had to be exhausted and terrified, but both of their faces held an almost blank look that worried her more than when they were crying.

They were in the back of a cargo van with no seats or anything to keep them off the cold dirty metal floor. A few times, the van turned a corner at such high speed, they be dumped into one side or the other of the van. Lyra had hoped Murphy might be pulled over by the police for his driving, leading to the chance for them to get help, but that hadn't happened.

The van came to a stop and Lyra heard the driver's door open and shut, followed a moment later by the van door opening.

"Get out." Murphy barked the order and Lyra expected the girls to jump in fright. They didn't and she didn't know if that was a good thing or a bad thing. They slid out and so did she. They were in the woods. An old cabin stood nearby, but there seemed to be nothing else around them. It was dark, with little light breaking through the woods, so she supposed it was possible there was another cabin right next door.

Somehow, she doubted it. The place felt isolated, lonely.

Murphy walked behind them as they moved toward the small building. Lyra held the girls' hands and barely processed the small squeeze Prentiss gave her hand. She felt the squeeze one minute, and the next Prentiss broke free and was running straight toward the edge of the woods.

Murphy cursed and raised his gun toward the fleeing figure. Lyra didn't have time to think. She screamed and launched herself, shoving as hard as she could, but he was too strong for her. He stumbled rather than falling, but turned the weapon on her and Alyssa, who had scrambled to clutch Lyra's arm.

Lyra backed up and turned to shield Alyssa, waiting for a blow, a shot, something to hit her. It never came. She turned to see Murphy swing his weapon back to where Prentiss had disappeared into the woods and Lyra grabbed for him again. This time, he struck her with a back-handed crack to the side of her head and her head swam as she went down.

"Fuck! Fuck!" Murphy watched the woods where Prentiss had disappeared and looked back at Lyra and cursed again. "You better pray she doesn't go far. Move it." He shoved Lyra toward the cabin.

Lyra's heart pounded and dread swamped her again. Everything in her wanted to race after Prentiss, to hold her tight and protect her. She was four years old and she was running blindly through strange woods in the dark. She looked down and saw Alyssa looking up at her.

Alyssa squeezed Lyra's hand just as Prentiss had done immediately before she ran. Lyra knew then the girls had somehow planned the move. She forced a shaky smile for Alyssa as Murphy pushed them through the front door of the cabin, but her heart was cracking and she'd never felt such a strong urge to fall to her knees and weep. She wouldn't, couldn't in front of her daughter.

Murphy continued to push and shove her as he moved through the cabin. She only realized as they entered the building that he'd grabbed a bag from the cab of the van when they got out. A backpack he now hung over his shoulders, switching the gun from one hand to the other as he did so.

"Up." He growled the words and Lyra saw the ladder in front of them leading to a loft.

"You go first, baby." Lyra moved to let Alyssa up the ladder, but Murphy grabbed Alyssa's arm and her daughter cried out in pain, before clamping down on the sound.

"Hell no. She'll climb with me. You first." His eyes were hard and the rage at losing Prentiss was apparent. But beneath it was something else. Fear. He was afraid.

Lyra guessed he was afraid of Damon. She climbed the ladder to find a small loft, hearing Alyssa and Murphy making their way up behind her.

"Try anything else and I'll shoot you both. I'll make sure

I don't shoot you dead, though. I'll make it hurt and I'll make you suffer." His threats came at her the entire time he worked his way with Alyssa up the ladder.

Lyra thought fleetingly of trying to hit him and knock him down the ladder, but the thought left as soon as it came. She couldn't risk that with Alyssa so close to him.

The pair crested the top of the ladder and Murphy thrust Alyssa to one corner of the room, pointing his weapon at Lyra. "Stay where you are."

Lyra raised her hands up and nodded, but her eyes flew to Alyssa. "Stay there, baby."

Murphy opened the bag and pulled out ropes and duct tape. "You better hope like hell I can find your other brat." He didn't say what would happen if he didn't, but he seemed to be unravelling a bit at a time. Each time he spoke, she sensed more tension in his tone wasn't. Maybe he'd screw up and she'd find an opening to get them out of there.

She winced as he pulled the ropes tight around her wrists, then bound the ropes to the leg of a low bed in the loft. The bed was anchored right to the floor. She guessed that was a safety measure and almost wanted to laugh. It wasn't turning out to be safe for her.

Murphy finished tying her up, put duct tape over her mouth, then went for Alyssa. Lyra couldn't stop the automatic response to seeing him near her child. She wrenched at the ropes, but he'd tied her to the leg of the bed without any slack in the rope. As she tried fruitlessly to pull free, she did nothing more than make her wrists raw.

Murphy pulled Alyssa over to the bed and Lyra's heart slammed in her chest. God, if he hurt Alyssa. Tears broke loose and streamed down her face, but he gave her a look that told her to sit still, and she did.

To her relief, he tied Alyssa to another leg of the bed and turned back toward the ladder.

"Don't try to get out of here. I'm going after your brat. You'd better pray I find her before Damon gets here. He'll do a lot more than tie you up if he finds out she ran."

CHAPTER TWENTY-SEVEN

The walls were closing in on Luke as he paced the apartment. They were back at Zach's place. Zach and Logan were now four hours north. They'd be closing in on Dartmouth soon, but they still had no idea where Damon would have taken Naomi.

Damon still seemed to have no idea Luke had infiltrated the group of buyers ready to bid on the Brain Trust's information the minute Damon pulled the trigger on the auction. Luke had received an alert to his fake account twenty minutes ago that the auction would be live in the next few hours and he need to be on standby if he wanted to bid.

They didn't have much time to mess around now. Samantha needed to turn her attention to trying to get into the account Damon had locked Billy out of so they could try to lock down the information before it could be auctioned off.

Luke suspected there would also be copies, likely a backup on a physical drive in Damon's possession. They'd need to get that, too, but first they needed to locate everyone.

He stopped pacing and sat across from Billy. "You've known Damon for years, right?" He kept his voice calm, even though he really wanted to wring the guy's neck. Billy had sat numb and useless since they'd gotten back from the recording studio.

"Uh huh. Since freshman year of college."

Luke nodded and rested his elbows on his knees as he leaned toward Billy. "All right. Let's walk through things bit by bit."

Billy winced. "Yeah. Okay."

"You guys went to school in Boston?"

Billy answered with another, "uh huh."

"Where did Damon grow up?"

"On the west coast. California. His dad raised him."

"Okay, good." Luke thought for a minute. They already knew Damon lived a few minutes from here in an apartment. They'd gone there after the recording studio and found it empty. Joel didn't own any more properties in the area other than the recording studio, and his office and home had been empty. Damon had no properties listed in his name.

"So, during the summer, did Damon stick around campus or did he go back to the coast?"

"He stayed in Boston. He worked. His dad didn't have a lot of money and he had to work to pay for his books and shit."

"What about someplace he might go with the girls? Would he take Lyra and the girls to someone in Boston? Maybe a place you guys used to stay? Or a friend's house?"

It was entirely possible Damon had taken Lyra and the twins with him to grab Naomi, but Luke had a feeling he wouldn't' want to do that. It was too unpredictable, too hard to control them while he snatched Naomi. Chances were, he and whoever was working with him had split up. They would stash Lyra and the girls with one or two of them while Damon went after Naomi.

Billy shook his head slowly. "No. I mean, I don't think any of our friends would keep quiet if he showed up with Lyra and the twins and was keeping them against their will. People liked him but . . . "

Luke waited as Billy seemed to chew on the idea for a minute. "Our friend Jeff has a place in Boston that he doesn't stay at very much. Jeff travels for work. He isn't married or anything, so his place might be empty. We've stayed in it before when we visit, even if he isn't around."

Luke looked at Samantha. She was watching them, waiting.

"Where is it Billy? What is Jeff's last name?" Jesus, it was like pulling teeth with this kid, Luke thought.

"Uh, Jeff Silver. I think the place is in Boston. Or right outside there. The street is something like Pineridge, Oak . . . something."

Samantha was clicking the keys. "I've got a few. Hang on." She clicked through more screens and hit the keys a few more times before looking up. "Pine Way in Newton, Massachusetts?"

"Yeah." Billy pointed at Samantha and nodded. "That's it. That's it."

"You got the guy's number?" Luke asked, tossing Billy his cell phone. When he got a nod from Billy he continued. "Text him. Tell him you're in the area and want to know if he's around to hang out."

They waited several minutes, and again, Luke thought those walls were getting closer and closer. The room seemed smaller with each tick of the clock. He needed to remind his brother to get rid of the damned clock on the wall. Who had a clock with actual ticking hands anymore?

Minutes later, a text sounded and Billy read from the screen. "Sorry, bro, out of town. Back in a week if you're still around?"

Chad and Luke exchanged a look. "It's the best lead we've got," Chad said.

"It's not much." Luke couldn't stand the idea of sitting still waiting, but he also hated the idea of getting further away from Lyra if she and the girls were still here. "Jax, can you stay here in case we're wrong?"

"Yeah. And I've got buddies in that area we can call if we need more people."

Luke gave him a grim nod.

"Billy, do you have a key to Damon's apartment?"

"No."

Jax stepped forward. "We don't need a key. I'll get us in." Billy looked up at him and Jax flicked his head at the door. "Come on. You're coming with me. We'll see what we can find in his apartment."

"Get me a credit card statement and his computer, if it's there," Samantha said.

"We'll call you with his credit card info," said Jax over his shoulder.

Luke and Chad followed. "Keep us posted, Samantha," Luke said, as he shut the door behind them and they all fanned out to follow leads that could be absolute shit.

CHAPTER TWENTY-EIGHT

Prentiss turned another rock on its side and leaned it against a stick, then kept moving. Her breath sounded loud in her ears, but she didn't think Murphy had followed her. She brushed at the snot and tears coming down her face, but kept moving. She knew enough to know she needed to keep moving, even if she wasn't able to stop crying.

When she saw a cabin in front of her, she slowed, being sure to mark the spot where she exited the woods with a large pile of rocks. She piled three, four, all the way up to ten, making sure she could easily spot it again when she left the woods and turned back to look.

Then, she ran forward, letting the tears stream down her face as she made a fist and hit the cabin door as hard as she could.

CHAPTER TWENTY-NINE

Naomi closed her eyes and hummed. *Christopher Robin and I walked along, under branches lit by the moon.* In her head, she heard her Uncle Luke's voice singing to her as they lay in her bed, looking out the window at the moon.

She ignored the hands on her body, focusing on the words that had become part of her heart and soul growing up. *So, help me if you can I've got to get back to the house at Pooh corner by one.*

The sound of duct tape being pulled from the roll broke through her thoughts and she squeezed her eyes shut tighter. His hands moved, pulling the tape around her rib cage. She wouldn't think of the wires and equipment she'd seen him lay out when he'd barked at her to raise her arms out to her sides. He didn't have the gun in his hands right now. If she were going to try to fight him, to try to run, now was the time.

Naomi opened her eyes. She couldn't pretend this wasn't happening any more. It was real. It was very much happening. *Chase all the clouds from the sky...*

They were in the back of an SUV. The man her uncle had called Damon seemed to know the area. He'd pulled off, following several side roads until they came to what seemed to be a broken down industrial area. There wasn't anyone around and many of the buildings boasted broken out windows.

The gun he'd held on her was next to his thigh on the seat, wedged with the handle facing up. He could grab it quickly. But right now, she'd rather fight and die than wear the bomb he was strapping to her. Once he got those wires connected, she didn't know if she could fight the panic of knowing he could trigger it at any moment.

Until then, he'd kept her bound in the floorboards of the car as they'd travelled for what she was sure was hours.

Naomi thought to the many self-defense lessons Luke had insisted on over the years. She felt shame she hadn't employed them earlier when Damon grabbed her. She'd just let her guard down at school. If anything, she should have been more on guard, but she'd been on guard to things like a frat guy slipping a drug into her drink at a party or getting caught walking back to her dorm alone after dark.

It hadn't dawned on her that someone would shove a gun in her ribcage in the middle of the day on campus. To her, everyone at college was simply a friend she hadn't met yet. When she'd heard her name, she'd turned to see who was calling her without giving a thought to how close someone was getting to her personal space or whether she was in a good bladed stance to have the balance to fight off an approaching attacker.

No matter. She needed to focus now. Naomi steadied her breathing as her captor twisted two wires together at their frayed ends.

She focused on relaxing her body before bursting to life

with one swift move. She brought her hands up and raked her nails over his eyes with all her might.

A howl broke loose from him and she shoved hard as his hand clutched for the weapon by his side. She tossed him off balance, then kicked with her feet before reaching behind her for the door handle.

Time seemed to drag in slow motion as she fumbled for the handle, then she was pulling it and she was half falling, half throwing herself out of the vehicle.

She found her footing as he screamed and she ran, toward one of the abandoned buildings.

CHAPTER THIRTY

Luke and Chad were making good time. They'd traveled more than an hour, mostly in tense silence, when Luke's cell phone rang. His heart kicked into gear when he saw a phone number he didn't recognize. In fact, he didn't recognize the area code of the number, for that matter.

"Hello?" He gave Chad a sidelong look as he answered.

"Hello, is this Luke?" The voice on the other end of the phone sounded like the person was older. A man.

"Yes, this is Luke. How can I help you?" Luke made sure his voice sounded even and steady before shaking his head at Chad's questioning look, giving him an *I got no clue* shrug.

"I've got your niece here. Says she's lost."

Luke's gut churned. He opened his mouth, prepared to tell the man to put Naomi on the phone. He didn't know how she'd gotten away, but he didn't care. If she was safe, that's what mattered. He didn't have time to speak when the man began talking again.

"Prentiss, she says her name is, but she didn't tell me

much more than that. Just raised up her shirt and showed me her Uncle Luke's number written on her back." The comment held a question and Luke didn't blame the guy.

He paused a beat before answering, putting the phone on speaker, so Chad could hear the conversation. Chad pulled off to the side of the highway and hit the hazard lights as he pulled out his own phone.

"She's safe?" It wasn't hard for Luke to put the right tone of relief in his voice. There was nothing fake about it. What was hard was trying to come up with a story that would keep the guy from getting the police involved right away. Luke needed to get to Lyra and Alyssa and give Zach a chance to free Naomi before they went after Damon. "Where is she?"

The man sounded relieved himself and Luke flicked through a few stories in his mind before settling on one as the man replied. "She wandered right out of the woods up to our vacation cabin. Been coming here for twenty-six years and we never had a child wander out of the woods like that. She says to us, 'I'm Prentiss. I need you to call my uncle.' Then she lifts her shirt and shows us your number right there on her back."

Luke forced a chuckle but it sounded choked. "It's a precaution we take whenever we're camping with the kids. Never needed it until today. Thank you so much for helping her," Luke said. "We've been worried sick." Not a lie.

"Well, we're over near Mount Monadnock. On the property on the west side of the pond."

"The pond?" Luke echoed. Chad was pulling up the map app on his phone.

"Rockwood pond." The man rattled off an address and Chad plugged it into the phone, tilting the screen toward

Luke. The map showed they were over an hour away, but they were closer than they would have been had they stayed in New Haven.

"I can't believe she made it that far," Luke improvised. "We've got a search party out but we thought she'd gone off the other way. I need to hike back out to my car and drive around to you. Might take me forty-five minutes or so. I also need to call off the search, let everyone know she's safe. Can she stay with you for that long?"

"Oh, you bet," the man said, and Luke prayed her captor didn't pursue Prentiss to this man's doorstep and hurt him. "My wife is making her something to eat right now. We're happy to keep her here with us."

"I don't know how to thank you, sir. Can I speak with Prentiss for a minute? I'd like to let her know I'm on my way."

Chad had already pulled back out into traffic and begun their altered route when Luke heard Prentiss's voice. He could hear her voice break a bit when she said hello, and the thought of what she'd been through speared him straight through the heart.

"Hey, sweet girl." He softened his voice for her. "Are you all right? I'm on my way to you right now, but I don't want you to say anything to these people about the men who took you for now. Can you do that for me?"

"Yes." She didn't ask why and he didn't want to explain that the last thing he needed was the police getting involved. If that happened, Damon would kill Naomi. It wasn't a risk he could take.

"Are you okay? Are you hurt at all?" He asked again.

"I'm okay." She paused and he could almost hear the gears running as her brain worked. She was crazy smart for her age. Hell, for any age. She amazed him. "I marked a trail where I walked, Uncle Luke. When I realized I was lost, I marked a path so you could see where I had gone," she said, and he understood her message.

"You marked the path from the cabin you're in to where your mom and 'Lyssa are?"

"Yes," she said. "A cabin."

"They're in a cabin also?" he asked.

"Uh huh. With Murphy."

Luke's gaze shot to Chad's. She'd just named Damon's partner. "Okay, baby. You hang tight. I'm coming. Just hang tight, okay."

"Okay, Uncle Luke."

CHAPTER THIRTY-ONE

"Damnit!" Zach hit the wall as he spun. They'd talked to Naomi's roommate and tracked down several of her friends. No one had spotted her and no one reported seeing Damon on campus.

Logan's phone rang and he lifted it to his ear. "Hey Sam, anything new? We haven't found any trace of Naomi here. However he got her, he did it in a way that didn't draw a whole lot of attention."

Zach began counting as he tried to calm his frustration. The detectives in his precinct all made fun of his counting, but it was what kept him sane half the damned time when a case got the better of him. Right now, he didn't know if he could ever count high enough to calm the anger building in him. He'd vacillated back and forth from anger to fear and back again on the drive up, but right now he was in full-on anger mode. He was more than ready to take out some of his emotions on the asshole who'd dared to grab his niece.

He made it to three hundred and eighty-eight before Logan hung up.

"Prentiss got away and made it to a cabin to call Luke. Apparently, Lyra was able to write Luke's phone number on Prentiss's back before she got away. Luke says Lyra and Alyssa are being held in a cabin. They're an hour out but headed that way." He went on to summarize the lead Chad and Luke had been working on when they'd gotten the call from the man who'd found Prentiss.

"So, they think we should head that way? See if Damon is taking Naomi to this friend's house in Newton?" Zach looked around at the campus. He hated the idea of leaving the area if Damon and Naomi were still there. If he was a television detective, he'd call his partner and have them run Damon's financials, see if the guy had used his credit card recently and track where he was that way. In real life, he'd need a warrant for that, not to mention more time than they had. Sometimes, real life sucked ass.

Logan seemed to be weighing their options as well. "No one's spotted her here. Could be he's headed south with her. Might be planning to meet up with Murphy where he has Lyra and the girls holed up."

"Or he could be headed to Newton."

"Or he could still be here." Logan gave the last possibility.

Zach stared at the campus green a moment longer, then looked back to Logan. "Let's head out. They're not here. We can head south and decide which way to go on the road."

Logan grunted as he turned to the car, and Zach knew what he was thinking. They were heading onto six hours missing and they had nothing. Without more to go on, they might as well flip a coin to decide where to head next.

CHAPTER THIRTY-TWO

Naomi's feet tripped as she heard a shot behind her, with a resulting ping that sounded like Damon's shot had hit metal. She veered, trying one door and finding it locked. The industrial park was isolated. She had no hope of running to someplace where she might find help. She needed to find a way to hide, then she'd come up with a plan. Maybe she could find a weapon.

Her breath came in panicked gasps as she turned and ran again, hearing footsteps closing in behind her. A window to her right was broken out and she dove for it, thankful it was low to the ground and large enough for her to wedge herself through. The packs of explosives he'd taped to her torso caught and she pulled and cried out as panic struck and pain sliced through her belly. The glass was cutting into her, but she ignored it and pressed forward, her legs following her through the opening.

With no time to let her eyes adjust to the dark room, she stumbled forward, banging her shins on something hard before dodging around it and heading toward a flight of wooden steps.

She heard a curse behind her and the sound of her attacker attempting to follow. She prayed the opening in the window was too small for him to fit through. It might slow him down if he had to find another way into the building.

The stairs creaked and moaned as she rose, and Naomi smelled urine. The building must be used by transients. She wondered if any of them might be here now. If they'd help her. If they'd fight off Damon and help her get to safety somehow.

At the top of the steps, she found a heavy door. Her hand closed on the knob and she tried to turn it, but it was locked.

A guttural cry escaped her and she shook the door, shoving at it. She needed to get out of the basement. Tears streaked her face as she threw her shoulder into the door.

Pain shot through her with the hit but the door didn't budge.

"Naomi." The voice came from further down the length of the building, a singsong taunt that told her Damon had gotten into the building and was coming for her.

Naomi pressed her lips between her teeth, clamping down on the sob that built deep within her. She couldn't afford to make any noise.

Her eyes had adjusted to the dark. She slowly descended the stairs, praying none of the stairs would squeak and give away her position.

He dropped the singsong and called out to her in the deep, threatening tones he'd used so far with her. "When I fucking find you, I'm going to make you wish like hell you hadn't done that. You and I are going to play, but I'll be the only one having fun. I'm going to make you fucking pay, bitch."

A shiver rocked Naomi's body as she crept through the dark. There were doorways at the end of the room. She headed toward them, wanting—needing—to put a barrier between her and Damon. Maybe she could find a weapon. Or maybe they'd lead to a way she could get out of the building. If she could get to another building, if she could hide or lock herself away from him long enough, he'd be forced to give up and leave.

He was on a timeline. She knew that much. He'd kept them moving. He was trying to get them someplace, though she didn't know where.

She reached the first door and moved through it. There was a small room and another door beyond that.

Locked.

Naomi's eyes swung wildly around the small space she was in. She couldn't risk going back out into the other room and running into him. He was too close.

Her heart sank as she realized she had blocked herself in. She was trapped. Everything in her screamed to sink to the floor. To curl up in a ball and close her eyes, squeezing them shut until this nightmare ended.

She couldn't do that.

The room was strewn with old desks and shelves, turned on their sides. She scanned for something to use to defend herself with. Her heart raced as she heard something fall in the outer room. It was close. Too close.

She moved to the door and crouched behind it, waiting as her breath sounded in her ears.

"I'm coming, Naomi," he called. "And then we're going to really play, you and me."

Naomi held her breath, straining to listen to his movements. She watched through the crack between the door and the wall as his shadow crossed in front of her.

Her heart beat in her chest and she counted the beats as it slammed hard against her ribs. *Three, four, five, six, seven, eight, nine...*

He stepped into the room. "Come on, girl, don't leave me hang—"

Naomi shoved the door as hard as she could. Damon went flying, his gun going down. She came around the door and ran for the opening but his arm shot out, grabbing her ankle, and she pitched forward.

A sickening crack sounded as her wrist hit the floor and pain shot up her arm and twisted her gut.

She scrambled, crawling forward, reaching. Trying to stand, to move, to run.

He was on her, hands fisted in her hair as he swore at her, slamming her head into the concrete floor again and again.

CHAPTER THIRTY-THREE

Lyra jumped when the door to the cabin slammed and she heard Murphy swearing a blue streak in the room below them. Alyssa's eyes went wide, but she remained quiet and still. They'd removed the duct tape from their mouths as soon as Murphy had left. Lyra wasn't sure why he thought they wouldn't be able to take it off, but the man wasn't all that bright.

Of course, he'd been bright enough to tie their hands so tightly she hadn't been able to get loose. In fact, her hands were numb and tingling from the pressure of the ropes.

Murphy was storming below them and she took a deep, smooth breath. He hadn't found Prentiss. She could tell. Her heart kicked and stumbled back into the right pattern again at the thought. Prentiss had gotten away.

Lyra took a deep breath and steadied herself. So far, she'd been trying not to remind Murphy that she and the girls could identify him, that they knew who he was.

But it was clear now he needed to change tactics. She needed to appeal to him and remind him that *he* knew *her*.

That he knew her and the girls well. That they weren't nameless, faceless captives to him. She had no idea why he was doing this, but this wasn't like him.

She licked her dry lips ad raised her voice. "Murphy. It's not too late to let us go. I know you don't want to do this. I can see it. Your grandmother wouldn't want you to do this either."

He went still beneath the loft and she hoped she had his attention, had him thinking.

"It's not too late Murphy. You can let us go and I can tell everyone we came here for a camping trip and Prentiss got lost. We just need to go find her. She'll come to me if she hears me calling and we can put this behind us."

Still nothing from Murphy.

She softened her tone. "Your grandmother wouldn't want this, Murphy. She wouldn't want you to do this."

"I did it for her," he said quietly, his voice breaking and thick with emotion. "It wasn't supposed to be like this. No one was supposed to be hurt."

Lyra heard the sound of soft sobbing from below. She prayed that meant he would help them. She needed to get her girls out of here before Damon came back. Somehow she knew, deep in her gut, that once Damon was back, there wouldn't be any getting out of this. "No one has to be, Murphy. Let us go and we can all go find Prentiss. I'll tell everyone we went camping. You came with us. She got lost and you helped me find her."

"I already found her," he called up.

Lyra's heart froze, dread whirling and circling through her in a dizzying sickening spin.

"You found her?" Lyra didn't look at Alyssa as she asked the question.

"She made it to a neighbor's cabin. She's inside with them. I couldn't get to her."

The relief that coursed through Lyra was so sudden and overwhelming, she felt flush and weak. Prentiss had made it to safety. Whether she got help to her and Alyssa in time, at least one of her girls was safe. It was a moment of hope in what seemed an endless stream of darkness.

The moment was short-lived.

CHAPTER THIRTY-FOUR

"Luke," Samantha's voice came through the speakerphone when they were minutes outside of the small town holding the cabin Prentiss had fled to. "Jax got me Damon's credit card information and I was able to get into his accounts online. It wasn't that hard. His login info was Qwerty and his birthday."

Qwerty was a common piece of passwords used by people too lazy to come up with something unique. It was basically the six letters on the top left-hand side of any keyboard. Adding his birthday did little to ward off a brute force attack at cracking it.

Sam didn't wait for his response. "Damon gassed up at a gas station thirty minutes from the cabin you're headed toward. The charge went through about forty minutes ago. He should be at the cabin by now."

Luke cursed. They were five minutes out from the cabin Prentiss was in and he still needed to track her movements back to where Lyra was being held.

"I've sent Zach and Logan your way, but they're behind

you by about an hour or more."

"Thanks, Sam." Luke disconnected. As much as he wanted backup, having Zach be so far away was a good thing. If he got caught up in what was about to go down, his career would be shot to hell. It was better for Chad and Luke to handle this and try to explain their way out of shit with the local police department after the fact.

He dialed the number for the man who'd found Prentiss and listened to it ring. He needed to buy some time so the man didn't get suspicious and call the police.

"Hello?"

"Hi, this is Luke Reynolds, Prentiss's uncle. How's she doing?"

The old man spoke softly. "She was really worn out. She fought it, but she's fallen asleep on the couch with my wife. I think once she warmed up and got some food in her stomach, she couldn't fight it anymore."

"Good." Luke was relieved to hear it. It was better Prentiss wasn't awake and anxious about her mom and Alyssa. And the man was right, she probably desperately needed to sleep right now. "Listen, we've hit a roadblock here. There's an accident they're working on clearing, but it's going to slow us down for a bit."

He apparently didn't sound as nonchalant as he thought he had. There was a heavy pause on the line, one thick with the knowledge that something wasn't right.

"Mr. Reynolds, I served in the 23rd Infantry for three years in Vietnam and that was only the tip of my service. I saw plenty of action before my retirement. I don't know what's going on, so I'm just going to tell you this. If you've got something you've got to go take care of, that little girl's going to be safe here with me. You rest assured about that."

Luke closed his eyes, thankful for his years in the

service in a way he'd never been. "Thank you, sir. I'll be there for her as soon as I can." He wasn't going to offer details but he appreciated the man letting him know.

Chad didn't comment, even though the phone had been on speaker. He offered a raised brow with a little nod and kept right on driving toward their destination. They had family to rescue.

CHAPTER THIRTY-FIVE

The door to the cabin flew open, slamming into the wall behind it, making Lyra jump from her spot in the loft.

Damon's deep voice echoed as he spoke. He shoved someone toward the couch on one side of the room. The woman's hands were bound and there was a hood over her head.

Lyra couldn't make out much from where she sat, but it only took Lyra a moment to process what was around her torso. Explosives. A lot of explosives.

"What the hell did you do, Murph? What do you mean the girl's at another cabin?"

Lyra held her breath and locked eyes with Alyssa. The little girl had fallen asleep for some time, but she was awake and alert now. Damon stood in the part of the cabin they could see from their position in the loft, but Murphy remained out of sight.

Damon's eyes were swollen and angry looking. Whoever he'd just brought in had fought him. Hard.

"Damon, man," Lyra heard Murphy say, "this isn't right. I didn't sign up for this. This is crazy. We can't—"

Damon strode forward, moving out of Lyra's sight, but the crack of a fist on flesh was unmistakable and Murphy's grunt of pain confirmed he'd been the one to receive the blow. As if it could have been any other way.

"We do this and we do it through to the end." Damon's voice was low and deadly. There was a kind of calm to it that belied the situation, making him all the more frightening. "There isn't any turning back now."

The last of this was said with the kind of sneer in his tone that said he'd listened to Lyra trying to talk Murphy into letting them go. Damon threw her words back at Murphy. *There isn't any turning back now.*

"Now, tell me where the hell the girl is."

Murphy relayed what had happened with Prentiss.

"You let a four-year-old get the better of you?" The anger whipping through Damon's voice seemed to lash at the air, palpable and terrifying. If Lyra thought she'd been frightened before, she was mistaken.

Murphy didn't try to justify his actions. "She's in a cabin a few minutes from here. I saw her through the windows, but she's with some people. We can't go after her, Damon. They're an old couple. We just need to let her go, get the auction done with and then take off."

Lyra could read Murphy's mind. He was thinking of his grandmother. He'd said he did this for her, but she didn't know at all what that could mean. Money. It had to be money, but for what, she didn't know.

Still, going after someone else's grandparents—innocent people who'd only had the misfortune to be in the wrong cabin in the woods when her daughter fled their captors—wasn't sitting well with Murphy.

Despite his obvious reservations, Lyra didn't have to wonder if Murphy had the backbone to stand up to Damon. She knew he didn't have it in him. He was done. They'd argued before, but Murphy had backed down at all turns, and she knew he would do the same now. He wasn't going to be the one to get them out of this.

"I don't give a fuck who the hell they are. You get over there and you take care of them. All of them. I'll run the auction from here and then we'll close this shit down and get to the boat."

There was silence. If Lyra wasn't sure he'd just told Murphy to kill Prentiss, she might have given more thought to the mention of a boat. As it was, her heart seemed to have fallen into her belly and she felt only an overwhelming dread at the thought of Prentiss out there and alone. Of Murphy coming to find her after she thought she was safe. After she'd thought she had escaped this hell.

"Go!" Damon shouted, and Lyra heard shuffling as Murphy presumably moved toward the door.

She closed her eyes. She was out of ideas. It was down to a miracle now. In her head, she pictured Luke.

CHAPTER THIRTY-SIX

Luke reminded himself to buy Prentiss an endless supply alarm clocks and DVD players to disassemble to her heart's content when he got them out of here. The girl had marked her path well.

How she'd kept her head and marked the path despite how frightened she must have been, he didn't know. He did know she was one hell of a girl, and he was so damned proud of her.

He and Chad moved through the woods from one pile of stones or sticks to another, being careful not to miss any in the dark.

Luke raised a hand to the near-silent Chad. The man had been an Army Ranger. Luke had always heard their ability to melt into the darkness, to hide in plain sight, was crazy, but the way that man could move his large frame through the woods without a sound was unreal.

Chad came up beside him and Luke pointed. Lights. The outline of a one or two room cabin ahead. And two cars in the open space in front of it.

Voices rose from inside, the heat in them making the argument going on inside the small space apparent. Good. If they were arguing, they would be off their game.

The door opened, light spilling out as a man exited. The door shut behind him before Luke could make out anything inside the space.

He and Chad moved back, splitting apart and taking cover in the brush.

The man raised his hands to the top of his head in a move that telegraphed frustration and slowly circled as though arguing with himself now. When he turned, the outline of the rifle on his back became more apparent.

For one split second, Luke swore the man was staring directly at them, but he looked away.

Whoever he was, he turned back at the cabin for a full minute, before cursing and heading for a spot in the woods not ten feet from Chad and Luke.

The look that passed between the two men was unnecessary. They backtracked silently, staying ahead of the man with the rifle as they circled to come around on either side of him.

When he passed between them, Lyra's neighbor's grandson didn't know what hit him. Luke stepped in to take him down and he and Chad carted the man off, away from the cabin, deeper into the woods. Deep enough to make him talk.

CHAPTER THIRTY-SEVEN

Wild eyes looked back at Luke.

"I'm going to take my hand off your mouth and you're going to keep it shut, you hear me?" Luke ground out.

Murphy Lawson nodded, as defeat and resignation washed over his expression.

"It's over, Murphy. The only way for you to help yourself now is to help us out." Luke eased up on the pressure on the man's mouth and Murphy nodded again.

It was almost comical how much Chad dwarfed Murphy as he held him, arms pinned at an awkward angle behind his back.

Luke let his hand drop from his mouth and stepped back as Chad continued to hold Murphy secure. "Are Lyra and Alyssa in the cabin?"

"Yeah," Murphy choked out. "And your niece. I swear to God. I didn't want any of this to happen. He said he just needed to scare Billy into keeping quiet. He said it was all for show. Things just got so out of hand."

Murphy was blubbering like a baby now, and it wasn't attractive.

"Damon? He has Naomi in the cabin, too?"

Murphy nodded.

"Tell me where everyone is." Luke needed positions and as much information as he could get.

"Lyra and Alyssa are tied up in the loft."

"Is it on the left or right side when you enter the cabin?" Chad asked quietly from his position behind Murphy.

"The left. Up a ladder. They're not hurt, I swear. I didn't touch them." His eyes flicked away from Luke and Luke knew he was lying. His blood turned to lava and rage tried to take over, but he shoved it aside. He'd give this guy so much hurt and pain when this is over for each hair that was hurt on his girls' heads. For now, he needed to focus.

"Where are Damon and Naomi?"

A buzzing in his pocket made him stop and pull the phone out. Another alert from Damon. The online auction had begun. Bidding would end in thirty minutes.

Shit. He hoped like hell Samantha was taking over for him. He'd given her his login and password and told her to bid whatever the hell she needed to. He was going to see to it that Damon was never paid.

He shoved the phone back into the pocket of his BDUs.

"Now," he looked back at Murphy with eyes he knew would tell the man he was running out of time. "Tell me exactly where everyone is in the cabin."

Murphy did, explaining that Damon had been on the lower level in the living room with Naomi on the couch at the back of the room.

"But, he..." Murphy seemed to stumble over his words and Luke felt a hard knot form in his gut. "He..."

"He what?" he growled. If Naomi was dead, he'd tear

this man's head off. To hell with the consequences. His niece was everything to him.

"He's got a bomb strapped to Naomi." The words rushed out of Murphy. "I swear to God, I didn't know anything about that. It wasn't in the plan."

This man was going to need to beg God instead of continuing to swear to Luke. Maybe God would have mercy on him. Luke sure as hell wouldn't.

Luke let his lips curl into the kind of feral grin he hadn't felt since he'd left the teams. "A bomb, huh?"

Murphy's nod was quick and Chad caught Luke's eyes and smiled.

Explosives. Now that was something a SEAL could deal with.

CHAPTER THIRTY-EIGHT

When Murphy had told them all he could, Luke and Chad secured him to a tree with materials from the Mary Poppins backpack Chad had slung over his shoulders.

They moved into place, with Chad heading up the side of the cabin to enter through the window at the top of the loft. Log cabin construction had the advantage of providing foot and hand holds they could use to their advantage. Of course, it didn't hurt that Chad's backpack also contained climbing equipment, ropes, and a small metal piston for breaking out the glass window.

Time to rethink his assessment of the man's addiction to gadgetry. Luke set the charges on the hinges of the door. He'd like to have body armor, but this would have to do. He moved around the side of the building.

Luke would bet Damon wasn't willing to blow anything up while he was still in the building. The man was too in love with himself to risk that.

Luke was doubling down on that bet, choosing to go straight through the front door using a small charge of his own as a distraction. A low whistle told him when Chad was in place outside the window. He would use the sound of Luke's small explosion to cover the sound of the breaking glass.

Luke froze. He could hear the quiet sounds of Naomi singing, her voice shaky. *Chase all the clouds from the sky...*

He closed his eyes. He'd sung that to her a hundred times. The memory washed over him as he opened his eyes and focused on what needed to be done.

"Shut the fuck up!" Damon's angry shout cut of Naomi's song and Luke took the moment to blow the charge.

In seconds, he was around to the front door and up, one swift kick taking the door the rest of the way down, weapon drawn on Damon.

"Drop it."

Damon stood halfway between the couch and a table where his laptop sat open. He held a gun, pointing it first on Luke, but swinging it back toward the couch. Murphy had been wrong. That, or he'd lied. Not that it mattered.

Damon had moved Lyra and Alyssa to sit on either side of Naomi on the couch. His niece's face was battered and bruised, blood crusting her chin and he swallowed against the urge to run to her, to assess the damage.

Luke burned at the site of the swelling on Lyra's face. He wanted to rush to her and hold her tight. All of them. He wanted to pull them all into him and whisk them out of there. Alyssa was the only one not banged up. Her precious eyes met his and he saw hope burning there. Hope and a fierceness that made him proud.

"Not gonna happen." Damon held up a small black garage door opener. "You shoot me and they're dead."

"That right, Damon?" Luke let a slow smile take over

his features and wondered if Damon had ever seen a man go down from a head shot. He would sink to his knees instantly, before falling over in a boneless heap. And that wasn't a dead man switch the asshole was carrying. If he wasn't alive to push the button, that thing wasn't going to go off.

That didn't mean he wanted to gamble on a clean head shot right now. Not until his backup was inside the cabin.

Luke kept his eyes on Damon who had begun to ease back to the laptop. He didn't look up, not letting his gaze give away Chad's position as he moved into place above them in the loft.

"The auction's not going to happen, Damon. We've got people working on shutting it down right now. They'll move in on your bidders before they know what happened."

It wasn't exactly true, but he was hoping Samantha would be able to gather information on each of the bidders so the commander could move on them. It would be a bonus if they could take down more than just Damon and Murphy. Of course, everyone in the Brain Trust who had shared confidential information gleaned from their positions could be facing charges, as well. At the very least, there'd be civil suits and their jobs would be shot to hell.

Luke glanced away from Damon quickly, letting his eyes take in the equipment strapped to Naomi's chest before moving back to Damon. He'd be willing to bet there wasn't a damned thing that was real on that device. Was he willing to bet the lives of the three people sitting on the couch? The ones who held so much of his heart and soul in their hands?

Shit, maybe not.

Damon sat, tapping on the keyboard, a look of panic crossing his features. Chad took advantage of the distraction to drop from the loft as Luke launched himself at Damon. The laptop went flying as Luke hit hard, taking them both to the ground as the wooden chair splintered beneath them.

He heard the gunshot as a bolt of fire pierced his side but he didn't stop. The pain didn't come close to touching him as adrenaline coursed through him.

Raising a fist, he slammed it into the side of the man beneath him, a satisfying crack resounding through the room. He saw his gun on the wooden floorboards two feet from where he wrestled with Damon.

He could hear Alyssa's screams behind him and he prayed Chad was getting her out of the cabin, away from the visions that would haunt her for a long time to come. Hell, he'd never expose her to this if he could help it. He wanted to shield Lyra and the girls from everything that might hurt them or cause them any fear.

As long as he lived, he would never get the sound of Alyssa's screams out of his mind.

Luke grasped Damon's arm and slammed it hard against one of the wooden legs of the chair until the man released his hold on the gun. Luke raised up, lifting his arm for another blow, but Damon shoved a hand into the wound in Luke's gut. Pain blinded him momentarily, searing heat plowing through his midsection.

Damon shoved hard, but Luke kept his leg out to the side, bracing against the smaller man's efforts. Luke shifted and rolled, grabbing for his gun to come up firing. One, two. Double tap to the body. Dead center mass.

Another scream told him Alyssa was still on the couch and Luke looked over as Damon fell.

Chad switched places with Luke, coming to watch over the man that bled out on the floor as Luke rushed to the three women on the couch.

A gurgling laugh came from Damon but Luke tuned him out. He didn't care what the man was saying. The asshole was likely going to be defiant to the end. He seemed to think the world owed him something, and Luke wondered where he'd ever gotten that idea.

Luke saw immediately why Chad hadn't gotten the women outside. Wires now ran from Lyra and Alyssa to Naomi, who sat stock still in the center. Tears streamed down her face.

Luke knelt before Alyssa and cupped her face between his hands. "Shh," he soothed, and his gaze jumped between all three of them before landing back on the littlest of them. He dropped his eyes to the bomb to double check before looking up to reassure her. "It's not real, sweetheart. The bomb isn't real. Superheroes know these things."

He didn't tell her it was his training as a SEAL that told him it wasn't real. Let her hold on to the idea of a superhero a little longer. Hell, she deserved it. "It's clay, baby. Just pretend, make believe, I promise."

Luke heard the trembling breath tumble out of Naomi as Lyra let loose a sob that damned near cracked his heart. He worked to strip them of the wires and the ropes that bound their feet and hands.

Alyssa leapt into his arms as he heard sirens in the distance and Naomi wrapped her arms around both of them. Luke looked up and found Lyra's eyes locked on his, tears running freely down her face. He reached out and pulled her toward him with one arm, bringing her close. He needed to smell her, feel her. To know she was there, alive, safe.

"You came," Alyssa said into his shoulder.

"Always. I will always come for you, 'Lyssa." The

promise was one he knew he would always keep. As long as he lived, he would be there for the twins.

"Prentiss ran." She pulled back for this part, eyes wide. "She went to get help for us."

"She's safe. She got to safety and had someone call me. She's not far from here. I'll take you to her." His eyes shot to Lyra's. "That was really smart to write my number on the girls. She was able to lead us right to you."

Alyssa spoke up again. "I think Wonder Woman has to talk to you now. You can probably get her to come see us now, I bet." Her mouth quivered but there was a grin splitting the girl's face and Luke took the first free breath he'd taken since getting the picture of them hours before on Billy's phone.

Alyssa looked up at Naomi. "He's a superhero."

"He really is, isn't he?" Naomi said, but it was Lyra that Luke was looking at now.

He soaked her in, needing to reassure himself she was okay as he heard the sounds of police arriving and Chad calling out that they needed an ambulance and someone to take two men into custody. His eyes stayed on Lyra's. She was the most beautiful sight he'd ever seen.

CHAPTER THIRTY-NINE

Luke took two seconds to text Zach and warn him off the scene before he took the women outside. Now that Zach knew Naomi was safe, he could stay away and save his career. No one needed to know a New Haven Police Detective had knowledge of what was going down and didn't call it in to his boss or alert local authorities once they knew the location of the cabin.

After that, they were all taken into custody. The women were taken to the hospital, along with Prentiss and Alyssa who hadn't let go of one another from the moment they were reunited.

Murphy, Luke, and Chad were taken to the local sheriff's station for questioning.

Damon was pronounced dead at the scene.

They didn't mention the auction. As far as the local police were concerned, Damon and Murphy had been involved in a kidnap for ransom scheme and Luke and Chad had rescued them.

When they were allowed to make a phone call, Luke dialed the Commander. Turned out, Samantha had already been in touch with him, though how that woman knew how to reach him was beyond Luke's understanding. Samantha Page was like that, from what he'd heard.

She'd been able to gather a lot of intel from the auction and she managed to get into Damon's accounts and keep the auction live while agents from several agencies prepared to move on some of the bidders.

Not all of the potential buyers were in the United States, and some of them couldn't be pinned down, but two homegrown terrorist groups—one a white supremacy group and the other a group that grasped onto any religion they could simply to be able to invoke it as the catalyst for causing violence—would be taken down.

Luke told the Commander that Damon mentioned fleeing the country by boat. How they'd track that boat or find out the details of that plan, he didn't know, but he'd leave that to the Commander to deal with. As far as Luke was concerned, Damon had to be a little crazy to think he could bury so many bodies and get away, but maybe he'd planned to spend the rest of his days in a country without extradition to the United States.

After that, it was surprising the speed with which things transferred from the local law enforcement to the feds. Luke and Chad were taken out of there to be interviewed two hours away at the nearest FBI facility. They were no longer being held on possible murder or manslaughter charges, but they had to be debriefed.

Luke waited in a small room he knew was used for interrogations, his body aching. They'd done a quick patch job on the worst of his injuries. The gunshot wound to his side had turned out to be a flesh wound. The bullet had grazed the surface of his skin only, though he'd swear at the time it had taken out a chunk of his abdomen.

What hurt the most was not knowing what was going on with Naomi, Lyra, and the girls. He had been able to see none of their injuries were life threatening before they'd left the scene, but that still didn't make being separated from them any easier.

He'd seen a look pass over Lyra's face when she'd looked at him as she was bundling the girls into the ambulance. A look that said she'd remembered his betrayal. Remembered that he'd used her, gotten close to her to bring her brother down.

The look had haunted him and he was beginning to think there was very little chance he was going to be seeing her again when this was over. The thought made his heart ache. He'd thought getting back into his career would give him purpose, but he was so wrong. The people in his life were what gave him purpose. And he might lose her.

The door to the room opened and the commander walked in, looking a little stiff and worn.

He sank into the seat across from Luke. "You sure as hell brought a lot of people into this."

Luke met his look with one of his own. "It was necessary."

The commanded nodded, but Luke couldn't read him. "Yeah, shit got a little out of hand, huh?"

Luke wasn't going to defend himself. He'd done what he had to do and the auction had been stopped. It was a good outcome.

"Listen, I don't know if you can do anything for him, but Billy Kemp wasn't in on the auction. He thought they were going to go to the companies with the information and sell it to them so they could patch their security leaks, not exploit them. Stupid, but the kid didn't know. As soon as he found out about it, he worked with us to try to stop it."

The commander leveled him with a look. "Oh yeah? Came and confessed to you, huh? Told you everything?"

Luke shrugged. "More or less."

"I'll see what I can do for him, but he should expect to serve some time."

Luke nodded. "He knows that. He's been helping Samantha and he'll help you guys with anything you need to know about the Brain Trust."

"I can find more work for you, if you're interested," the commander said, after a beat.

Luke supposed he must not be all that disappointed in the way Luke had handled things. The commander rubbed at the back of his neck and Luke saw the years of responsibility for the lives of thousands—hell, millions—weighing on the man.

When the commander spoke again, his tone was heavy. "There are other threats we're looking at right now."

He didn't specify, but Luke didn't need him to. "I think I'm going to pass. I need to see to some . . . things." It was a lame response, but it was the truth. He didn't know what he wanted.

Months ago, he'd thought he wanted back in. That fighting for his country, diving back into the fight for what was right and what was wrong, was the way to bring meaning to his world.

He had a feeling he was wrong. Meaning was sitting in a hospital room right now. And he wasn't sure she'd forgive him.

CHAPTER FORTY

Luke shook Chad's hand outside the hospital entrance. "Thank you isn't enough."

"It'll do." The big man grinned and walked around the driver's side door with a wave. He'd be heading back to his wife and kids, and Luke couldn't deny the ache that banked deep in his chest.

He was jealous. He wanted that.

Luke raised his hand in a wave before turning to the hospital entrance. Zach greeted him in the hallway.

"Naomi's up on the third floor."

Luke nodded, feeling a little numb. "And Lyra and the girls?"

"They're on five. Pediatrics. Lyra wouldn't let them check her in. Insisted on staying with the girls, so they treated her injuries up there."

"He didn't . . . she wasn't . . . " He didn't know how to ask if Damon had violated Naomi in other ways. If he had, Luke would crawl down into the bowels of hell and drag the man back so he could kill him more slowly.

"No. She wasn't. He didn't touch her in that way."

Luke let out a slow breath. It looked like Damon got to stay in hell.

Zach had already told him Naomi had needed some stitches on her abdomen and the back of her head. She'd be staying overnight so they could be sure she didn't have any serious complications from her head wounds.

He was sure if Lyra would let them, they would have insisted on the same for her, but she was a mama bear to the core. Her girls could come first.

His gut pitched as he wondered if Lyra would ever forgive him for using her and her girls to get close to her brother.

They took the elevator to the third floor. Luke wanted to kill Damon Taylor all over again when he saw his niece's battered face. She was bruised and one eye was almost swollen shut.

Tears sprang to her eyes and her hand went to the back of her head when she saw him. "They shaved my hair."

Luke walked to the bed and wrapped his arms around her. "I'm so sorry, Naomi. I never meant for this to happen."

Her voice broke when she spoke and he felt tears on his bicep, where she'd turned to bury her head. "I knew you'd come. I knew you'd find me."

"Always." He answered with the same promise he'd given Lyra's girls, and he meant it.

He held her as she cried and rocked her like he had when she'd been young. The idea that he might have lost her because of some inane need to get back to a career he'd long ago left gutted him. What the hell had he been thinking?

Naomi pulled back and wiped her eyes. Luke got a look at the back of her head, where they'd shaved off her long dark curls to stitch up her wounds. He put a hand to the side of her head, where the hair remained.

"It'll grow back. In the meantime, you'll set a new fashion trend or something."

She gave him a disgusted grunt, the kind she reserved for times she wanted to remind him and Zach that they lacked the estrogen necessary to understand some things. He wholeheartedly agreed with her, as he had many times before.

"Have you seen her?" Naomi didn't have to tell him who she meant.

"Not yet."

"You need to go to her."

Luke offered Naomi a small smile. "Yeah, I'll go see the girls soon. Just as soon as I talk to your doctor. Make sure you're all right."

They'd need to make plans for her to take some time off school while her head healed, he thought. She'd fight him on it, but he wanted her at home where he could keep an eye on her. At least for a little while.

"No." Naomi shook her head, then winced.

"You okay?" He came close again. "Where does it hurt?"

She took his hand. "I'm fine. I promise. But, listen to me. You need to go see Lyra. You need to talk to her, explain to her why you were there and—"

He cut her off. Lyra might understand why he'd done what he had, but it didn't mean she'd be able to get past the betrayal of it.

"She's going to go back to her life, and I'm going back to mine, Naomi," he said quietly, and he'd swear a knife arched through his chest as he said the words.

Naomi leaned toward him in her hospital bed and Luke

saw Zach step forward protectively on the other side of the bed. "I know you, Uncle Luke. I saw you falling for her. I saw how happy you've been the last few weeks. You don't need to give that up."

Luke didn't look at Zach, even though he felt his brother's eyes on him. "I lied to her Naomi. Everything I said and did with her was a lie. There's no coming back from that."

She took his hand and her gaze was steady. He was so damned proud of the woman she'd become. "You can come back from this. You can make it work. Just talk to her. You always told me we can get through anything together if we just keep talking to each other through the good and the bad."

Luke nodded. "Yeah, all right, sweet girl. I'll talk to her." He wouldn't, but there were times he'd realized, parents needed to lie to their kids.

He squeezed her hands tight before releasing them. "I'll go up and see her." He looked to his brother. "You'll stay here?"

Zach nodded. "I got this."

Luke took the elevator to the fifth floor and walked the length of the long hallway.

He froze when he rounded the corner.

Lyra stood in the hallway with an older man and woman. He didn't have to guess who they were. The girls' grandparents. Prentiss and Alyssa came out of a nearby room, catching sight of him. Squeals rang out as they ran toward him, and Luke went through the now familiar act of kneeling to catch them. His heart ached as he did it, the feel of small arms wrapping around his neck. Lyra looked down at the floor, when he tried to catch her eyes, and he knew. He just knew, she was going to say goodbye.

He couldn't blame her. He held the girls a little tighter

and breathed deeply as they buried their heads in his shoulders.

Alyssa was the first to pull back and the absence when Prentiss followed was palpable.

Luke reached out and tugged on Prentiss's pigtail. "I'm so proud of you, Pren. You were so brave to get help."

"Did you find my trail?" she beamed with the question.

"I did. Couldn't miss it." In reality, she'd done a damned good job of leaving clues that anyone might walk right past. It was only because he'd looked for the small piled of stones and sticks that he'd seen them.

"We're going to Nashville with Nan and Pop!" Alyssa bounced on her toes and her resilience floored him.

Prentiss piped in. "There are six nonstop flights a day. We get to fly."

Luke looked to Lyra and stood. He offered his hand to the older couple.

"The girls have been telling us all about their personal super hero," the woman said. "I'm Willa Hill and this is my husband, Jerome."

Willa Hill was tall and thin with short cropped gray hair and skin a deep rich brown. Beside her, Jerome matched her in height, but his hair held only a hint of gray at the temples.

The man offered his hand next. "We owe you a debt of gratitude, young man." His shake was firm and strong, but there were tears in the man's eyes.

Luke simply nodded. The man didn't owe him anything.

He cleared his throat and looked to Lyra who seemed to be looking anywhere but at him. She watches the girls as they swung from his hands.

"Nashville, huh?"

She nodded. "For a little while. Just to—"

"We're going to take care of these babies." Willa's arm went around Lyra, squeezing her shoulders tight, as though Lyra were one of the babies, too, and Lyra smiled at the tall woman.

Luke opened his mouth, wanting to say something, but before he could, Savvy and Tracy came down the hall. There was another flurry of hugs and tears, and telling of tales by the girls. Luke moved to the side, thinking he could wait until her friends' attention was on the twins and then pull Lyra aside to talk. Although, what he would say, he wasn't sure.

He didn't get the chance. A nurse broke up the group, walking between them all and leading everyone back into the hospital room.

"Okay, I've got the last of the paperwork, Mrs. Hill, and you'll be set to go."

Lyra glanced at Luke as she walked away, but her eyes quickly shifted away and she was gone.

CHAPTER FORTY-ONE

Lyra smiled as Savvy wrapped her arms around her and hugged. As much as she'd needed the time away at her in-laws, three weeks was a long time to go without lunch with her girlfriends. They'd gotten the scare of a lifetime when Savvy had come to the apartment in the middle of the night and found Lyra and the girls had disappeared suddenly.

"We missed you!" Tracy said, taking over the hug where Savvy had left off.

Lyra smiled. "I missed you guys, too." She sat on the couch as Savvy took the other side of it and Tracy took the large chair beside it.

"So, tell us. How is the business going?"

Despite the fact that Joel's business had survived, she had given her notice right away after the kidnapping. She realized she needed to grab life and go after her dreams. Dream Weavers for Women had been born two weeks ago.

"I'm booked for the next four months." Lyra couldn't believe her launch had gone so well. She offered branding and software solutions for women-owned businesses. Within days of her launch, several friends had posted about the business in a few Facebook groups for women-owned businesses, and things had grown from there. "Now I have to sustain it."

"You will," Tracy said with a wave of her hand. "Word will spread and you'll be turning people away for years to come."

Lyra grinned. Despite her happy expression, there was an emptiness she'd found she couldn't get rid of. And its name was Luke. The man had left a gaping hole unlike anything she'd felt since she'd lost her husband years before.

"So, Billy took the plea?" Savvy asked.

"Yes. If my parents hadn't stepped in and paid for a solid attorney, I don't know if he would have gotten such a great deal. It helped, too, that Luke and Samantha told the FBI he worked to help them stop the auction."

"How long will he serve?" Tracy put in.

"Three years in a minimum-security prison." Her heart hurt just thinking about Billy in prison, but he'd known what he was doing was wrong. He had to face the consequences for the choices he'd made.

There was a pause and Lyra didn't miss the look Tracy and Savvy exchanged. She raised her brows at them.

"Have you talked to Luke?"

Lyra shook her head, a tight knot forming in her throat.

"We were wrong." Savvy was the one to speak but Tracy was nodding her head.

"What do you mean?"

"He wasn't a hot quick lay to keep you busy while he was here," Tracy said.

"What she said." Savvy pointed and nodded. "He cared about you. We could see it as soon as we saw you guys together."

Lyra shook her head and fought the rising tears in her eyes. "I was a job to him." She felt the stab of warring emotions. Humiliation, anger. Want.

"That man had feelings for you. I don't care what his job was or what brought him here."

Tracy jumped back in. "He wouldn't have gone to bat for Billy as much as he had if he didn't care for you."

Lyra bit her lip and looked back and forth at the girls. "I don't even know where he is."

Savvy let out an offended huff. "You have his phone number. Getting in touch shouldn't be all that hard, even if he isn't across the hall anymore."

Lyra let her gaze fall where her feet rested on the coffee table.

"What are you afraid of?" Savvy asked her.

"Everything."

"That's a little vague." Tracy swatted at Lyra's feet with one of her own. "Explain."

"I just don't know if I can go through that again. I mean, I thought I could. I thought I was ready to open myself up again, you know? And then I found out he's some under-cover cop or something. In the end, I realized, it wasn't betrayal that hurt so much at that moment, it was the thought that he was gone. That I didn't really have this great new thing in my life."

"This is one of those dance things."

"Huh?" Lyra looked at Savvy and couldn't help but smile.

"Sure, those dance things. That's the song. Actually," Savvy frowned. "It's a lot of songs. *I Hope You Dance,* and that one by Garth Brooks about not having the dance even if there was loss that came with it. This is one of those dance things. And you, woman," she pointed her finger at Lyra, "deserve to dance."

Lyra nodded. She wished she could say she was feeling the confidence of a prized fighter, but the truth was, she wasn't. When she thought of facing Luke and having him reject her, she froze up.

Which was silly, really. She'd just started her own business. She was raising her twins on her own. She was a strong woman.

Lyra took a breath and felt hope flicker in her chest. "I'll call him."

Her friends' grins matched and they started to theorize about the reunion and how hot it would be. Lyra was laughing when she went to answer the door moments later.

CHAPTER FORTY-TWO

As soon as Lyra looked through the peephole, her heart rate skyrocketed. Luke stood on the other side of the door.

"Maybe it'll include wall sex." Savvy was still talking about the hotness of the reunion with Tracy as she fanned herself. "I've always wanted a guy who'd push me up against the wall and—"

"Shh!" Lyra cut her off and opened the door. She could hear her friend's hushed comments in the background, and she was pretty sure there was some ooh-ing and ah-ing and one mention of making popcorn.

"Hi." Luke glanced through the door at her friends, but then his eyes found hers and she saw just as much uncertainty in them as she'd been feeling. "Can we talk?"

Lyra nodded and stepped back as Tracy shoved Savvy toward the door. "We were just leaving." So, it must have been Savvy who'd made the popcorn comment.

When they had shuffled out the door, Lyra shut it and turned to Luke. She'd be lying if she said her head wasn't a little caught up on Savvy's up-against-the-wall sex comment.

He looked good. Really good.

"Hi," she said.

Intense eyes burned into hers and she felt her breath catch as she waited for him to speak. She'd missed him so much. Had he been feeling the same way?

He opened with, "I wanted to try to explain."

Her heart fell. He was just here to try to assuage his guilt.

"You don't have to, Luke. You were just doing your job. I get it."

"No. I wasn't. I could have done my job just fine without getting so close to you." He stepped to her with those words, one hand coming up to cup her face and slide into her hair, tipping her face back so she looked him in the eye. The other hand slid to her hip, pulling her close and making her heart slam in her chest. "That part. That part was all me. All because I wanted to be with you."

"Oh."

His thumb brushed her face. "I missed you."

She closed her eyes and took a deep breath, letting the scent of him seep into her. He was really here with her. He'd come back to her when he could have simply walked away. "I missed you, too."

His mouth was soft and yearning when he kissed her and she pressed into him. His arms came around her, pulling her close now and she sighed. This felt right. Good.

So good, like coming home.

He pulled back and rested his forehead on hers. "Can we start over, Lyra? Can we date and talk and get to know each other without the case between us? Please?"

She nodded. "I'd like that. A lot."

This time, when he kissed her, there was heat and passion and she responded so quickly it was almost dizzying.

Maybe she should have slowed things down then, done as he suggested and gone on a date. But she didn't want to. Her feelings for this man flowed deep. She pulled him closer, leaning to press her body against his and he growled his response. He back-stepped her into her apartment and shut the door behind her.

"Are we alone?" He asked, barely breaking contact with her mouth as he spoke.

"Yes." She ran her hands down his muscled back. "For several hours."

She thought she heard him swear but his mouth had moved to her neck and she lost all sense of what was happening. His hands ran down her body, bringing her to life beneath his touch. She was lost then, in sensation and emotion.

He lifted her and carried her to her bedroom, making swift work of their clothes when he arrived.

"You're so beautiful, Lyra. So soft, so gorgeous." The words were punctuated with kisses and nips as he came down over her, covering her body with his and working his way over her, learning her body.

She did the same, using hands and mouth to explore, to find out what made him tighten and groan.

When they came together, him entering her in a slick powerful thrust, their moans mingled and her heart tightened in hope, in the beginnings of love. In what she knew was a future that was more whole than what she'd dared imagine for herself in a very long time.

EPILOGUE

Nine months later

"They really love it." Lyra, Savvy, and Tracy stood shoulder to shoulder in the backyard of Lyra's new home. She was renting it, but they were out of their apartment and into a home with a backyard. Someday, she'd buy.

"They really do." She watched Luke push the girls on the swing set as Tracy's and Savvy's kids climbed to the top of the slide. Naomi stood by, talking to her uncle. She'd come home for a long weekend.

"And they love him," Savvy said, her elbow nudging Lyra playfully.

Lyra sighed. "They really do."

"So do you," Tracy said.

"Can't argue with you there." The women laughed and sipped their lemonade. Lyra had known she was in love with Luke for a long time. It was something that thrilled her and filled her days with wonder. Between Luke and her girls, her life was full.

In a little bit, there would be more friends coming over and burgers and hotdogs would go on the grill.

She saw Luke stop the girls' swings and lean down to whisper something to the twins, his gaze falling on her as he did. She didn't know what it was, but Alyssa and Prentiss slid from their swings and ran to her, smiles and laughter filling the yard.

"Luke says he has a question for us, Mommy," Alyssa said, taking one of Lyra's hands, as Prentiss took the other.

"An important question." Prentiss stressed.

"Does he?" She looked up to see Luke coming toward her, his eyes locked with hers as he reached into the side pocket of his BDUs. Naomi stood by his side, and he kissed the top of her head before she came to stand near Lyra and the girls, a broad smile on her face.

Lyra's breath caught and she heard her friends still beside her as he dropped to a knee. He held out a jewelry box that held a diamond ring in the center. The ring was flanked on either side by two smaller versions of the ring in just the right size for her girls.

"Lyra, Alyssa, and Prentiss," he said as Lyra's eyes filled with tears and her heart overflowed with love. "Will you marry me, girls? Be my girls forever? Be all in with me, as I am with you?"

Lyra pressed her lips together and nodded as the girls squealed and climbed into his lap. "Yes," she said, as he lifted the twins, one resting on either forearm, and came toward her. She pulled him in to kiss him.

"I love you," she whispered. "All in."

"All in," he replied. "I love you, Lyra. So damned much."

Later that night they lay together, moving slowly as he entered her and made love to her. It was different than the times he caught her in the middle of the day and held her against a counter or tabletop to make love to her. It was different than the times they'd lay in bed while she rode astride him, taking her pleasure as his hands dug into her hips and he roared his release.

This time was slow and sweet, it was love and honor and the knowledge that they would share a lifetime of this together.

As Lyra lay in Luke's arms afterward, her heart feeling like it might overflow, she looked at the ring Luke had placed on her finger. It was perfect.

"Please tell me the rings you gave the girls aren't real," she said.

The deep rumble of laughter that came told her he understood her girls. "No. But I did have real ones made. They're in a safe deposit box for them for when they're older. Along with three backup fake ones for when they lose these ones."

She laughed. He knew her girls.

"Hey, Lyra," he said, his mouth going to her neck as he shifted and came over the top of her.

She looked into his eyes. "Yes?"

He trailed a kiss along her shoulder before nuzzling her neck in the spot just under her ear. The spot that always made her moan.

"You've given me two girls."

"Mm hmm," she half murmured, half moaned.

"But I was thinking, I don't have any boys."

The laughter was lost on her lips as he brought her back to that place where words didn't matter. All that mattered were the feelings and emotions and sensations of her and Luke coming together. Again.

The End

Thank you so much for reading ALL IN! If you liked the characters who came in to help Luke toward the end of the book, check out my Sutton Capital Series and On the Line Series for their stories. You can find details at http://loriryanromance.com/books/.

The Sleeper SEALs series is a multi-author branded series which includes **twelve standalone books by some of your favorite romantic suspense authors.**

The next book up is **Geri Foster's BROKEN SEAL** and you can find it here: http://sleeperseals.com/series-books/#jp-carousel-50.

Check out the rest of the books at:

Susan Stoker – PROTECTING DAKOTA – 9/5/17
http://sleeperseals.com/series-books/#jp-carousel-39

Becky McGraw – SLOW RIDE – 9/26/17
http://sleeperseals.com/series-books/#jp-carousel-32

Dale Mayer – MICHAELS' MERCY – 10/3/17
http://sleeperseals.com/series-books/#jp-carousel-31

Becca Jameson – SAVING ZOLA – 10/17/17
http://sleeperseals.com/series-books/#jp-carousel-30

Sharon Hamilton – BACHELOR SEAL – 10/31/17
http://sleeperseals.com/series-books/#jp-carousel-34

Elle James – MONTANA RESCUE – 11/14/17
http://sleeperseals.com/series-books/#jp-carousel-38

Maryann Jordan – THIN ICE – 11/28/17
http://sleeperseals.com/series-books/#jp-carousel-33

Donna Michaels – GRINCH REAPER – 12/12/17
http://sleeperseals.com/series-books/#jp-carousel-48

Lori Ryan – ALL IN – 1/9/18
http://sleeperseals.com/series-books/#jp-carousel-49

Geri Foster – BROKEN SEAL – 1/23/18
http://sleeperseals.com/series-books/#jp-carousel-50

Elaine Levine – FREEDOM CODE – 2/6/18
http://sleeperseals.com/series-books/#jp-carousel-51

J.m. Madden – FLAT LINE – 2/20/18
http://sleeperseals.com/series-books/#jp-carousel-52

26993464R00121

Printed in Great Britain
by Amazon